the name on your wrist

www.totallyrandombooks.co.uk

the name on your wrist

HELEN HIORNS

CORGI BOOKS

THE NAME ON YOUR WRIST
A CORGI BOOK 978 0 552 56952 1

First published in Great Britain by RHCP Digital in 2013,
an imprint of Random House Children's Publishers UK
A Random House Group Company

This edition published 2014
1 3 5 7 9 10 8 6 4 2

The Random House Group Limited supports the Forest Stewardship Council®
(FSC®), the leading international forest-certification organisation. Our books
carrying the FSC label are printed on FSC®-certified paper. FSC is the only
forest-certification scheme supported by the leading environmental organisations,
including Greenpeace. Our paper procurement policy can be found at
www.randomhouse.co.uk/environment.

MIX
Paper from
responsible sources
FSC® C016897

Set in 11/15 pt Carré Noir Medium by Falcon Oast Graphic Art Ltd.

RANDOM HOUSE CHILDREN'S PUBLISHERS UK
61–63 Uxbridge Road, London W5 5SA

www.randombooks.co.uk/childrens.co.uk
www.randomhousebooks.co.uk
www.randomhouse.co.uk

Addresses for companies within The Random House Group Limited
can be found at: www.randomhouse.co.uk/offices.htm

THE RANDOM HOUSE GROUP Limited Reg. No. 954009

A CIP catalogue record for this book is available from the British Library.

Printed and bound in Great Britain by CPI Group (UK) Ltd, Croydon, CR0 4YY

For Hannah,
who was patient with my impatience
and listened to the endings
from the very beginning

1

The Reign of Tom III

It's the first thing they teach you when you start school, before they teach you to wipe and flush after you use the loo and before they teach you how to answer the register. But they don't need to. Your parents tell you when you're first learning how to say your name; it's drummed into you while you're taking your first stumbling steps; it's your lullaby when you can't sit up by yourself. By the time you start school the lessons are redundant. It's fully integrated into your psyche. From the moment it first appears, you don't tell anyone the name on your wrist.

Over the years, I've come to accept that human beings are incredible.

When humans are hot, their skin produces sweat which

then evaporates off the skin to cool them down, then that affects your pee. Salt too. All these mechanisms balancing each other out. The body is an intricate web of systems all designed to keep a couple of chemical reactions working, and all this biological science nonsense is encased in something that you can hug. Humans have eyebrows to stop sweat dripping into their eyes. Everything has a purpose. Each human body is a miracle.

I like bodies. I like thinking about the fact that, beyond the superficial surface of my skin, there's haemoglobin carrying oxygen and carbon dioxide; and the fact that that's possible due to ligand substitution, which all boils down to a matter of attraction and particles. It really makes you think, to know that while you're a person with a conscience and a mind, you're also just a delicate machine with the adequate mechanisms to cope with quite a few changes. If the changes are too big, of course, then you might get sunburn, or die.

I don't, however, like people.

People are unpredictable and predictable at the same time: it seems that whenever you want someone to surprise you they remain themselves, and those who were actually OK screw themselves over some way or another. People make stupid decisions on a regular basis but, worse, have stupid reasons for those decisions – because people are broken then forced together again in ways that they were probably never intended to be.

It would be better, I always thought, if people existed purely on a physical level rather than on the more complicated emotional, spiritual levels that came along too.

In short, Tom Asquith needed to go.

As a boyfriend, he was largely passable; he liked routines and he liked the appearance of things. So, I would be taken to dinner and paraded down the corridors in a way that was almost demeaning and almost flattering, depending on what sort of mood I was in. He asked me how I was and he genuinely seemed to like me – perhaps not as much as he liked the concept of having a girlfriend and the vague prospect of self-gratification, but that didn't change the fact that the entire thing was based on a lie. Well, more than one lie actually. I was a completely different person with Tom than I had been with Tomas previously (and Thomas before that), and the fact our relationship was based on a lie had never been directly stated but more *assumed*. I supposed it was closer to a notion; a metaphysical lie, which I found almost more insulting. As if he didn't have to waste his words on me – I was stupid enough to believe blindly.

My name wasn't written on Tom Asquith's wrist.

The trouble is, there's quite a lack of Corins, and when people think they're in a relationship with their soul mate they act differently – as if it's something precious, something sacred that must be upheld with honour. I've always thought that's the reason for the statistics they shove down your throat in those magazines – that soul-mate relationships have a less than one per cent chance of failure, compared to the much higher statistic for other relationships. It's the idea of obligation, really. If my name appeared on the raised, slightly red skin on his wrist, then he would have paid more attention to me in our earlier years of school, or he might have put a little more dedication and effort into an amazing present for my nineteenth birthday – imagining, no doubt, telling our future children about the first gift he ever bought me. Really, the perfume had been OK, but it was hardly a story.

With soul mates, it was *all* about the story.

And so Tom Asquith had provided me with the perfect get-out clause – what an arse.

I'd skipped school to read a book in bed (staring at the screen on my tabloid had been more than enough effort spent for a Monday, I thought) and as predictably as ever, Tom had turned up on my driveway in his antique car declaring that he'd missed me and asking if I'd wanted to get away before Jacinta turned me in and the shit hit the fan Motherwise. Affirmative, basically, and after he bought me a crappy dinner at a restaurant where he got a discount thanks to one of his mates, he'd parked up in the car park facing the beach to 'talk'. It wasn't so much of an estimate as to where he thought the whole evening was headed, as a prophecy. If anything, that made it more fun.

I liked letting people down. Particularly Tom, who had enough respect for me to do his best not to look too disappointed when I pushed off his hands or pulled away when he tried to kiss me, but lacked the emotional complexity to mask his feelings sufficiently. His half-irritated, half-desperate expression was actually my favourite of his collection – something about the corners of his lips seemed to be horribly affected by gravity, and it took him genuine effort to wrench his lips into a smile. He had quite a few expressions that I thought I truly would miss, but I was sure another Thomas would soon enough materialize to tend the wounds of my theoretically broken heart.

With Tom kissing me from the driver's seat, it would be very easy to decide to forget it for another week. I could wait for the following Monday (Tom wasn't particularly original – recently I was beginning to feel like my whole life was on repeat; that was mostly why it was now time for him to sod off and leave me alone) to reactivate the plan all over again. There were enough books to download to keep the whole routine going for at least another month, but I didn't want to exhaust my supply all in one go and, really, it was for the best.

If I let this continue, there'd be another jilted male wandering around school referring to me as she-who-puts-out and, frankly, I could live without Jacinta ratting me out to Mum about that. It would be easy enough to play the whole thing off as having my heart broken by multiple Thomases, but acting took effort and dedication.

'Hey,' I muttered, grabbing hold of Tom's wrist and threading my fingers through his, 'we should go back soon.'

Tom, with his face inches from mine, didn't look particularly convinced by this line of argument; he reached forward and kissed me again, pinning my hands against the window behind me. Tom's car was one of those archaic vehicles where gearsticks were still added as a sentimental, nostalgic feature that did nothing functional but were supposed to make the car feel vintage. It suited Tom, with his ridiculous love of appearance and lack of appreciation of the practical. He liked the fact that the world thought we were soul mates, even if he knew we weren't. He thought it made him interesting –

and Tom Asquith was anything *but* interesting.

Still, from the angle of things and the fact that he was concentrating on moving over to my side of the car without injuring himself on the fake-gearstick, it was easy enough to dig my nails under his wrist guard and access the clasp, twisting it free. Social etiquette didn't stretch to the behaviour of potential soul mates in the privacy of their own car, and given that we were now at the age when the search was supposed to begin, it was a perfectly valid and almost fair move. All the better for my reputation at school in the harsh light of morning — not that that had ever stopped me before.

The history books said that, traditionally, on their wedding night soul mates should take off their wrist guards for the first time. I don't believe a large proportion of what's printed in my history books, mostly over-exaggerated crap, but there's still a lot of superstition about that — that you shouldn't sleep with someone unless you've seen the name on their wrist.

I've never been great at following rules.

Tom kissed the spot of skin just under my ear and whispered something that sounded a little like 'I love you' at the exact moment that I let the wrist guard slide, turned the palm of his hand over and read the name printed there.

Teana.

Now that was interesting. The raised, red skin on Tom Asquith's wrist spelled the name of one of the least popular girls in school, who was at the very bottom of the social food chain (cruel, but then teenagers are always cruel). So it was little wonder that popular, well-thought-of Tom would have wanted to avoid that for as long as possible. I was his current distraction against what could potentially be the rest of his life: Teana Briggs, who, despite her social standing, was one of the nicest girls I'd ever met, who'd cut all her hair off and sold it to charity and whose parents were so strict that she wasn't allowed to so much as think of searching before she was a legal adult. Tom was certainly rebelling against their expectations, if she was the right Teana.

'Oh,' I said, freezing and shrinking away from him, eyes widened in a perfected expression of shock. 'Teana?'

'Corin,' Tom muttered, jerking back, hitting his hand on the gearstick in a rush to shove his wrist guard back into position. 'Look, I can explain.'

People felt naked without them fully covering the name. Uncomfortable. Unnatural. Pretty amusing, providing my own wrist guard remained firmly in place.

I didn't like seeing it either. I'd never seen someone else's wrist before and the image of it burned at the back of my memory.

'How?' I demanded, voice twisting into the hysterical as I hurried to unlock the car and push the door open. 'What, you just . . . you had a name transplant yesterday and forgot to mention it?'

'Corin!' Tom said, grabbing my arm and trying to stop me from leaving the car. 'Corin, you can't go — you're miles away from home, you just . . . look, let's talk about this.'

'There's nothing to talk about!' I said, voice still hysterical. The perfect balance of upset and angry.

'I didn't mean . . . I didn't mean to make you assume—'

'Yes, Tom, you did.'

'Just get in the damn car.'

'I'll get the train,' I said, letting myself start to cry (God, if acting was still a viable career choice rather than a monument of history, I would have been paid billions). 'I don't . . . I can't look at you right now. How could you? After my sister . . . ?'

The mention of Jacinta had exactly the desired effect: Tom blanched and suddenly looked disgusted at himself, uncomfortable, guilty and upset all at once. It was funny, the way my sister could affect my boyfriend's emotional well-being far more than I was capable of doing.

'I can't let you get the train. Those things . . . they're empty. Corin, come on. I can't do that to you.'

'You were going to do much worse,' I said, shoving my hands in my pockets to keep them protected from the January cold. I stalked away from the car, towards the train station. Tom called something after me (might have been 'I love you', and if it was, I didn't know whether to hit him or feel sorry for him), but I ignored it and took the steps down to the beach.

The beach. A place I did not want to think about.

At least there was (admittedly freezing) air down there and I liked the feeling of the wind whipping my fringe away from my face, even though I felt more vulnerable that way. There was no one watching (except perhaps Tom, if he'd climbed out of his car and was thinking of following; but I doubted he would) so it hardly mattered if I looked more like a kid than usual.

I'd liked the sea, but after my father died Mum hadn't

wanted to be constantly reminded of him every time she took a breath of air. She'd moved to the coast with him, being a landlocked sort of child herself, never dreaming that the Walden she was searching for went surfing for fun and spent his childhood eating fish and chips out of crisp sheets of recycled paper. She said that she'd never liked salt on her food, liked it less in the air she breathed and that she couldn't possibly stay at the seaside now. Back then, we weren't going to argue with our mother's strange state of grief. We just accepted it, allowed her to uproot us and added the beach onto the list of things to mourn.

We only moved twenty minutes away, it was true, but that was enough to ensure that she never ended up back here again: as soon as people have finished searching, they live small lives with few people in them. The world is only big when you're searching; once you've been found you can lose yourself within the fact that you belong with someone.

You're not supposed to need anyone else.

I took in one last indulgent breath of air before I snapped myself out of it, savouring the feel of the sand under my shoes as I began the walk along the beach towards the train station. There was a road that led in the same direction, and I'd probably get there quicker, but these days they only ran the trains when there were enough people wanting a ride anyway, so I doubted it would make much difference. If I missed one, all it would take was a sob story and a bit of mild flirting with the train driver before he commissioned another – simple.

This wasn't exactly my first late-night train ride back

home. The crude, large metal machines had a certain charm in their ugliness. While everything new seemed to be made of light, precisely balanced sheets of metal, the trains were solid and raw. A bit ridiculous, really. A hyperbolic machine of over-proportion and excess.

Everything had gone exactly the way I had planned it. Admittedly Mum would no doubt be angry for a little while before I explained the situation with Tom (more tears might be required for that), and Jacinta would goad me for hours, just because I'd given her ample reason to, but otherwise everything had worked out perfectly. I might skip school tomorrow in the name of heartbreak as I expected the Corin people saw outwardly would be quite devastated by the fact that she'd fallen for another rogue Thomas.

My thoughts jarred for a second and I paused on the steps back up to street level, just across the road from the train station. My breath caught in my throat as I stared, everything feeling rawer and more real than it had in weeks. After a few long seconds I managed to catch hold of myself, melting back into calmness before bursting back into motion.

Just a moment of weakness. A temporary state of insanity, thanks to staying up late planning how to undo my ties to Tom number three. But, still, there it was.

For a split second I thought I'd seen my ten-years-dead father.

2

Incident, Rumour

I decided I was too damn tired for the heartbroken charade when I finally made it back to my house — if I was exhausted enough to start seeing my dead father across the street then I certainly wasn't in a position to force myself to start crying about my wounded soul. Instead, I let my mum work herself up into a tip-top performance of disappointment and resignation about me staying out so late before I trooped off to bed in shame. Naturally there were things I could have done to prevent such a scene, as she pointed out: I could have contacted her to let her know where I was, but the 'my TTC went flat' excuse rolled off the tongue with such ease that it was barely worth the extra thought and effort. Never mind that being without a TTC was illegal — Mum expected these sorts of things from me.

Still, I liked letting my mother down as much as I liked letting anyone else down. I always felt like I was teaching them a valuable sort of lesson, imparting knowledge so to speak, because there's nothing like a huge disappointment to make you realize that your expectations are stupid and un-attainable; nothing quite like having your trust shot to hell to make you aware of the limitations of humanity. And given that no one listened when I told them that, it was just so much easier to show them.

One person who did understand was my sister, the messed-up and embittered Jacinta, who woke me up the following morning when she was entirely ready for school to inform me that we had to leave in five minutes. The sub-sequent rush in the bathroom was probably helpful for perfecting my broken-heart status, but it also meant that I didn't even have time to brush my damn hair (having only just managed to clean my teeth, which was obviously a priority) before Jacinta reappeared to darken the doorstep of my bathroom with a small smile playing across her features.

God, my sister was a piece of work.

I wasn't sure when our relationship descended into piss-ing each other off as much as humanly possible, but now I could barely remember a time when we were actually nice to each other. Either way, it wasn't unusual for her to switch off the alarm on my tabloid to ensure that I had to spend the day avoiding mirrors.

'I'm driving,' I muttered as we left the house together, Jacinta pressing the button to lock the front door as I stuffed half a slice of bread into my mouth and chewed. Awful stuff that Mum had cooked herself. One day, she'd give up the attempts to emulate blissful domesticity; until then, it was badly cooked food all round.

Jacinta didn't answer, but headed to the passenger seat anyway. She didn't like driving much, so I hadn't expected her to counter my assertion – I don't think she liked having control of something that could potentially kill. Cars weren't like how they used to be, so it was actually pretty impressive for a driver to succeed in doing anyone any damage – get too close to the path of a car with a TTC and the speed started dissolving – but I suppose you could still hurt yourself plenty. Our father was the non-living proof of that. Having that kind of power was just too much for my sister, apparently.

Our friends from the psych ward tried to pass this off as some lingering issues with cars after our father's death, but it hadn't actually been until after Jacinta's meltdown that she'd objected to cars. They just liked finding excuses for Jacinta's nonsense.

I pressed my head against the back of the driver's seat and took a deep breath. Now it seemed like it might have been better to explain to Mum about the death of another era of Thomas last night, because she would have undoubtedly let me take a day off to get over the trauma and I really didn't feel like facing the Education Centre. Not that that was new.

Jacinta leaned over and pressed her thumb against the recognition pad and the engine kicked into life. Bloody annoying anti-theft device, employed by my mother as the strictest form of punishment. Despite the car actually belonging to me, one late-night making-out session with Tom while parked on the front drive had led to my fingerprints being removed from the car's system, leaving me unable to start the engine without my sister's cooperation. I'd always thought it was dumb: it just encouraged car thieves to cut off people's fingers to use as a bloody sort of key. I'd rather lose my car and keep my thumb.

'Not skiving again like yesterday?' Jacinta asked pointedly as I reversed out of the drive.

'Told Mum about that yet?' I returned, glancing at the road and tightening my hands over the steering wheel. 'Or saving it till I'm out of the dog house for staying out late last night?'

'There's no need to keep *anything* about you saved up,' Jacinta countered, flipping down the mirror and frowning at her reflection, 'as you'll screw up again just as quickly.'

I swore at her distractedly, my thoughts catching on my sister's expression upon facing her appearance in the mirror — it was the same expression she used when looking at me, actually: one of utter loathing. Sure, neither of us had exactly inherited classic beauty or pretty features, but that didn't mean it was something worth getting upset over — we were striking, as my mum always said. Didn't make a damn bit of difference to get upset over it, anyway.

'Put the mirror away, Jacinta,' I said out loud. 'Don't need anything else in this car broken.'

'Hilarious,' Jacinta replied in a dark whisper, shutting the mirror with a clunk, folding her arms and then receding into herself. It used to scare me when she first started it, but now

I took it as a well-needed respite from our perpetual bickering; it was like she had a *power off* switch and when she didn't like the present any more she just shut down completely. Her eyes turned to this weird, harrowing shade of death, her lips twisted into a straight line and she was just not there as a person any more. I've never asked where she goes when she's like this, because quite frankly I don't care.

She must like it there, though, because she spends half of her goddamn life sat still as a statue, unresponsive to anything until she chooses to resurrect herself. There's a transitional in-between state which she takes on during school hours — one where she can answer questions in class, walk down corridors and conduct overly polite conversations without really registering where or who she is. I call her states of mind 'dead', 'robotic' and 'hell'.

It was for the best, really, because although her dead and robotic states weren't particularly alluring, she was much more amiable when she wasn't being herself. Harsh, maybe, but still true. 'Hell' was a state of mind that only I was blessed with and I had to love her by default. I just about managed it.

I plugged my TTC into the car and flicked through all the transmission waves until there was something almost decent to listen to. I don't even like music, when it comes down to it, but whenever I get within a five-mile radius of school I'm conscious of the need to start acting — most of the vapid teenage girls here liked to give the impression of worshipping music and I couldn't be bothered to attempt to defy the stereotype.

Anyway, it distracted me from Jacinta's hollow expression quite nicely. I could hate the electronically generated beats instead of hating my sister. Less barely concealed angst and questions lurking behind a hatred of techno.

The school car park was as full as ever, but it still struck a chord with me. I blamed skipping Monday and therefore managing three whole days of absence from the place, but it seemed ridiculous that there should be so many people here and yet Jacinta still ate lunch alone every day. It wasn't like I had any friends, either, but I saved up all my people skills for whichever Thomas I was currently dating – I couldn't deal with people, whereas Jacinta *needed* people in her own way.

'Jacinta,' I muttered, surprising myself by speaking up when I hadn't really intended to. The usual routine consisted of me abandoning her in the car the second the engine juddered to a stop, but now she was blinking herself back into reality and staring at me with those wide eyes. This was a real spanner in the works. 'I broke up with Tom last night.'

'So?' Jacinta retorted. The word felt particularly harsh, but I was used to this sort of violence just hidden below the surface of our conversations.

'Just thought you should know,' I said, pulling my bag onto my shoulder and pushing the door open, 'so you don't find out from someone else.'

'I don't care about your sex life, Corin,' Jacinta spat, opening her own door and switching over to robotic in one smooth movement. I watched her walk towards school for a few minutes to give myself time to compose my features and remind myself of who I was supposed to be – Corin

Blacksmith, nineteen, half orphaned, yet to be streamed into a career, with an older sister with a hundred different attitude problems. Or, more precisely, a heartbroken Corin Blacksmith who'd just been messed around by yet another guy, damaged goods, naive and a bit stupid, every bit the kid-teenager.

Tears would help with the whole charade but I was too dry of emotion to conjure up anything with quite such dramatic results. I closed my eyes for a second, head against the steering wheel, before deciding to go for a pseudo I'm-trying-to-be-strong act. Mostly because I was lazy and couldn't be bothered to think of anything more complicated than that, but partially because there was only so much I could stand people insisting on believing I was weak and vapid. The patronizing advice got old very quickly.

I detached my TTC before removing myself from the car too; bag on my shoulder, forced smile on my face, shoulders squared up to face the day. Exactly like normal, then, really.

It was a special talent that really irritating people had: being able to whisper louder than most people were able to shout. I was always torn between thinking the perpetrators were aiming to be heard, subconsciously knowing something was going to hurt me and increasing my hearing ability and, of course, good old-fashioned paranoia.

Lidea Crackmore had the most carrying voice I'd ever had the misfortune of being whispered about in. Worse than that, her insults weren't very original and I'd heard most of them at least five times today. It was Lidea's comments, though, that suddenly began to spark up proper levels of irritation in my stomach. I had a high tolerance for irritating things due to living with Jacinta and my mother, so instead of actually getting angry at people I tended to simmer until I was allowed to blow up in the space of my own room – but then people were being *genuinely* more ridiculous than normal today. I was owed an opportunity to scream and swear at them – it would be so very satisfying.

I'd known that the dramatic ending to my relationship with Tom would place me firmly in the heads of the school's resident gossips, but I hadn't banked on this level of participation from all sides.

I'd seen Tom three times already. He was waiting for me outside my first class, which meant I'd had to take a detour to the Further Education part of the Centre to escape him following me and that had led to me walking into the *first* Thomas. As far as I was concerned, Thomas Brooks was such ancient history that I placed him at about the same level as the Egyptians, yet I'd ended up facing him in the middle of the corridor for an uncomfortable, unplanned staring contest before I'd pretended to burst into tears and made a break for the girls' toilets.

Just after lunch I'd seen Tom Asquith talking to Tomas Prandle (Tom number two) and then I'd written off the day as a humungous mistake – it certainly hadn't been part of the plan to be haunted by ghosts of Thomases past, and I was still convinced that they were about to form some sort of Corin's-exes support group and walk around wearing badges declaring 'I was the wrong Thomas'.

Then, with the promise of biological sciences class being a Thomas-free zone, I'd dared to hope for a chance to breathe. Naturally that led to Lidea Crackmore conducting a very loud whispered conversation about me.

'If I were her,' Lidea whispered, 'I'd transfer schools.'

'Where to?' Jenny Johnson asked in return, perfectly logically. 'It's not like there's anywhere else close by.'

'Her *and* her sister.'

I turned round in my chair and sent her a vicious look, folding my arms over my chest and trying to restrain my tongue from saying something cutting and harsh — not because I cared about Lidea's feelings, but because more reports of me having a 'bad attitude' would delay the moment when I'm finally streamed even further.

'Or she should just stop dating until she knows it's an anima–vinculum situation,' Jenny countered. 'She must feel awful, though, being played again.'

My lips curled slightly at the sound of the Latin: *anima-vinculum* — the romantic's word for 'soul mates' with a literal definition of 'soul bond', which was both overly sentimental and dipped down into the idealistic. The only redeeming merit for something so fluffy and heart-warming is the fact that, linguistically, it's a really pretty phrase.

'She can't exactly demand potential datees to take off their wrist guard first, can she?'

'No.'

'And Tom made out like she was his carpinomen. And, from what I heard, she did see his wrist.'

'Reckon she'd tell us who it was?'

'I wouldn't,' I put in, turning round to face the pair of them again with my eyebrows raised slightly. 'Not that I owe anything to him — it's just, with how loud you two whisper, I think they'd overhear.'

It was doubtful, considering Teana Briggs wasn't in this class or even currently in this building (being clever and dedicated, she'd been streamed to 'doctor' almost as soon as she'd turned sixteen — she now spent most of her time in the 'hospital training' part of the Education Centre, which was pretty damn far away from the Level Four science subsection), but it would only be about ten minutes before the whole world was aware of the unlikely potential pairing and it'd make the poor girl uncomfortable. Plus, I liked having my shroud of secrets — it protected me.

Lidea's eyes doubled in size and then the two started to whisper with renewed fervour. I was betting that by the end of the day everyone would be convinced that either Jessica Standing or Billimena Dowse were going to become the future Ms Tom Asquith.

At last, the lesson ended and I pulled my bag over my shoulder and left the classroom as quickly as possible.

In terms of intelligence, I was way above Level Four science classes, but the Education Centre was adamant that I was not well-adjusted enough to be streamed — when they'd decide what job I'd be training for — so I was not allowed to progress any higher. That meant I'd covered so many of the classes offered at Level Four that they could easily pigeonhole me into any career they liked. And still I was left to rot with a mix of the stupid and the young.

When I was feeling particularly bitter, I blamed Jacinta for that. They didn't really like younger siblings overtaking their older siblings, education-wise, and although Jacinta was apparently considered more well-adjusted than me (bullshit, if ever there was any), she still wasn't allowed to progress any further than FE level. The system might think it was kind to prevent Jacinta being reminded of how royally she'd screwed up by stopping me from overtaking her, but it was cruel for me to be stuck in the bloody system, every damn day, because my sister was a first-class nut job.

I accidentally walked into Josaphine Woolgrave in my rush to get out of the classroom and she offered me a knowing sort of look that made my stomach turn. Any contact with her made my skin crawl.

Damn, today really was like walking through a messy concoction of the past and the present. Both were depressing.

None quite as depressing as the concept of the future.

There had been a time, before my dad died and before Jacinta turned into the monstrous creature that she was now, when I'd actually been relatively sociable.

At age four I'd been invited to start attending the Education Centre for basic pre-level classes, providing my parents considered me ready to begin what was essentially school. Jacinta, who was two years older than me, had received her invitation before her fourth birthday and was doing just fine, so my parents agreed that four was old enough for me to enter the first stream of education.

Josaphine, or 'Josa' as she insisted upon, had been invited

at the same time. My first day preceded hers by a week, so when I was appointed the task of being her 'friend' until she settled in, I'd considered this entirely beneath my levels of sheer intelligence (I'd practically mastered typing, by then), and of course that led to a three-year-long feud. The system doesn't think much of students who actively don't get on with each other, so we were pushed into all the same classes and seating plans until we cracked and gave in to what they wanted — friendship.

Except, our friendship wasn't as docile and safe as they'd predicted or wanted. We considered our first tabloids awesome, but our plug-out TTCs — transportable tabloid communicators — as tracking devices (I stood by that now, because TTCs embodied Big Brother, and I didn't like the government having that much knowledge of my life). We'd take out the batteries or leave them in the toilets, then run off to some part of the Education Centre where no one was able to find us and spend the day whispering about things. It wasn't technically against the law not to have a working TTC on you at age seven (that law kicked in at age twelve), but it was highly frowned upon and led to both of us being separated and prevented from starting Level One classes until we were beyond ready.

After producing the most exuberant friendship of my life they then set about trying to destroy it, bit by bit.

As it turned out they shouldn't have bothered. Josa confided in me, and in return I had to confide something to her. Those were the rules of our naive eight-year-old friend-ship, except back then I had so little to confess. My parents were happy, my big sister was a regular little genius, and I was pretty content too.

I didn't have anything to match the fact that her parents were asexual soul mates: that her dad was actually gay and she'd been produced through artificial means. That they were actually just two really good friends (anima-vinculum friends, the absolute truest form of friendship) who were bringing her up.

I had to give her something in return.

There are some things that, when you know them, are impossible to forget.

And it tore our friendship to shreds.

Onomastics and etymology (O&E) was one of my favourite classes. The fact that it was so specialized in itself meant that the Level Four class wasn't unforgivably dull, although I was still top of the class by a long way. Even a promised hour of O&E wasn't enough to cheer me up after such an abysmal day.

In some streams of FE the course had a requirement of continual widening of the knowledge base through Level Four classes and, being the beginning of the month, a whole new section of students had been promoted to FE (and I should have been with them, damn it) and were now dipping back into lower-level classes to meet the course requirements. Four new students meant the time-old introduction class.

Our first names would be entered into the worldwide name database on Mr Robin's tabloid. The class results would appear on the tabloid and our individual results flashed up on our TTC within about ten minutes. It was a program he'd written himself, connected to the database and synched up to all our TTC signals, but he'd only tell you that if you asked. If not, he was happy to let us assume he'd just downloaded it.

I knew my individual results by heart these days: 'Corin' was in the bottom two hundred names worldwide (although variations such as 'Corinne' were more popular), and the majority of Corins lived in either England or America, with approximately a hundred Corins in England. The statistics assume that your soul mate comes from the same country, which is distinctly more likely but not a definite, which basically means this: somewhere in the country were a hundred people with 'Corin' written on their wrist. Those hundred people were desperately searching for any Corin that might have their carpinomen too.

One of those hundred was searching for me.

And it was my prerogative to make damn sure that I was as difficult to find as possible.

'At the bottom again, Corin,' Mr Robin said with a grin in my direction. Predictably, the class results showed that my name was the most uncommon in the room. They also usually threw out the exceedingly low likelihood of one of the other members of the class being my carpinomen. Or, if you prefer, soul mate.

'I like being on the bottom,' I returned with my own smile, which caused Mr Robin to laugh and shake his head slightly and several other class members, particularly the new ones, to stare at me as though I'd grown an extra limb. 'With Colton on top, as per.'

'You don't hold it against me that my parents are vastly unoriginal?' Colton Furnish asked, lazing back in his chair and dragging his dark gaze over to me: he was my age, already boosted up to FE levels and had started this course last month. He was good at it too.

'It's hardly your fault,' I said kindly, with only a hint of sarcasm. 'At least your search is likely to end the day you start it.'

'Only if his carpinomen is as common as his own,' Mr Robin interjected, 'so, name a popular girl's name, Mac-Donnell.'

'Amy,' Oakley MacDonnell returned, turning round and raising an eyebrow at the resident Amy in the classroom.

Amy was in second position and looked embarrassed. At fifteen, she was extremely smart and probably wasn't used to being subjected to poor attempts at flirting from guys like Oakley. That was the problem with streaming and only moving up classes when considered 'ready' – they didn't factor in things like bad flirting and crude remarks. Only intelligence and emotional maturity counted – that is, emotional maturity as measured by the streamers, which isn't always accurate.

If anything, to survive in most Level Four classes you needed emotional *im*maturity to stop losing faith in all of humanity. An ability to laugh at bodily functions was considered a needs-must for Level Three classes, whereas in Level Four classes it was all about sex jokes. Poor girl was likely to be traumatized by the time she'd completed the course.

Mr Robin put 'Amy' and 'Colton' into the database.

'Estimated two months' search time,' Mr Robin read out with a grin, 'but you'll probably wind up with the wrong Colton and/or Amy.' He paused. 'Let's run it again, but a bit differently this time,' he said, addressing the class with that easy teacher way of his. 'Our resident bottom position with our top student — Corin with Colton.'

Colton leaned further back in his chair and quirked up his eyebrows at me as the rest of the class started cheering and generally making a lot of noise. I smiled back in response and folded my arms over my chest.

'EST . . . six months,' Mr Robin read out, 'which just goes to show, class, that it's not all about how common your name is. It's how common a pairing the carpinomens are.'

I liked Mr Robin. As much as his introductory class was recycled on a regular basis, he had a way of injecting something fun into what could potentially be quite a dry subject. That's the thing about streaming, though: if you get the right people on top then everyone is placed in the perfect job. More than that, you get exactly the number of people you need for each job — if there's a nurse shortage, just stream more people into the nurse courses; an overload of cleaners, push people away from that career path. Kills ambition, of course, but it means you don't have to worry about it. They tell you what to do and then you do it.

They told Mr Robin to become an O&E teacher and here he was, lamenting the fact that there were thousands of different contributing factors to how long your search would be — throwing out the fact that there was likely a reason for how long you searched for too, as if fate was one of the more significant of those contributing factors.

'So,' Mr Robin continued with a flourish, indicating Colton and me, 'although, as far as statistics go, it's unlikely that these two could be anima-vinculum, the reality is much kinder than the stats — fate.'

Well, that's one word for it.

Then Mr Robin's tabloid flickered off our class stats and each of our TTCs buzzed into action, because there was a news bulletin. As a mass of people, we all shifted in our seats slightly and waited to find out what the news was.

And it told us that someone had killed themselves — in the D'livere.

3

To the Hospital

Around sixty years ago, an old historic monument was knocked down. Sustainability was the word and, as much as all the world's historians were turning in their graves (or, more likely, their ashes were causing a stomachache to whichever poor sod had breathed them in), it was costing an entirely extortionate rate to keep the monument in place. The site had, before that, been home to an even older monument of some sort, and then one particularly mad historian had popped up stating that, thanks to a successive series of large buildings on this one particular site, it was likely that no one had ever died on this piece of land.

Personally I've always thought that whole concept was ridiculous. Every year they got more historians to track further and further back in history to determine whether it was true or not, and the historians always came back with the same result — that they thought it was entirely possible that the piece of land had, in fact, escaped death.

In a world where we seemed to have discovered everything and fallen into the most organized period of history that had ever existed, death was the only thing we couldn't escape. But, as the legend had it, there was still a piece of our ancient earth that *had*.

They roped it off, realized that wasn't enough, created a huge Perspex dome around the place to keep out any wild creatures that might wander inside and die, and opened it to the public as a place of healing and immortality. Once a year, the media exploded with a firestorm of coverage about it — hiring mediums who claim, shockingly, that the whole place is silent; finding those who swore the site gave them good luck and vitality. The oldest person on the planet usually features for a few moments, talking in an accent too thick for me to understand about how she regularly visits the place. Everyone takes a school trip to visit, despite the fact that it's on a different continent and people rarely travel these days. Everyone's been to the D'livere.

Of course, you had to have a note from a doctor stating that you're healthy and not about to drop dead and ruin the world's dullest tourist attraction. The organization involved in that school trip was ridiculous and, after all that — the flights, the passports, the check-ups — I didn't get to see anything of the American Section. It was straight back on the plane home and that was that. We travelled halfway across the world to stand in a Perspex box: and that's just one of the reasons why I've always hated humanity — the criminal lack of judgement and perspective. Perspex, indeed.

As we all took in the news, the whole room was silent. We'd all been there, so we were aware of the security imposed there. It had seemed over the top, then — why would anyone want to break into a stupid Perspex box?

Obvious, really. I wasn't sure how my thirteen-year-old mind had missed such an obvious point. *To kill yourself.*

The girl and her suspected soul mate had visited the attraction together. She'd put the knife in her wrist guard and then she'd slit her wrists. There was a video too, which showed a blurry image of the two entering the attraction together and then cut off to the scene outside the attraction. The news reporter was talking at the camera with a serious expression: they'd tried to remove the body from the area before she could bleed to death, but the guy she was with caused a commotion which distracted the security, so she died, right there, in the middle of the D'livere.

I wondered if it had felt good. Knowing, just for a second, that she was the first person ever to die there. The world's so old now, there are not a lot of firsts left. Just a lot of recycled ideas and a horrible lack of originality. Even in her case, I doubted that she was actually the first, but that was what the world was saying. She'd be remembered. She'd made her point.

The tabloid turned back to black, but the moment hung around the room for a little longer — all our eyes fixed towards the front, the tension and a sense of disbelief still hanging in the air.

It was hard to believe. It had been a stupid legend — but now it was over.

After a few seconds of respite, the inevitable happened. Over half the pairs of eyes in the room darted towards me and took in my stiffened posture, my tight smile and my angry gaze. Even Mr Robin succumbed to the urge, which was disappointing, an expression of pity and worry hitting my cheek for a second before it relented.

He seemed to come to, faltered back into speech and continued talking about search times and onomastics. Gradually the rest of my classmates pulled their gaze away and left me to my solitude.

Except Colton Furnish. He continued to stare right at me, unabashed.

Then again, there was nothing particularly unusual about that.

Jacinta was not sitting in the passenger seat or the driver's seat when I was finally allowed to escape into the car park. Normally she arrived at the car several minutes before I did and it was unusual for me to have to wait, but given the events of the day I wasn't wholly surprised — I supposed someone committing suicide in the D'livere was enough to drag anyone out of an emotionless state. Especially Jacinta.

I leaned against the bonnet of the car and tried not to worry too much. The effects of the news bulletin were still obvious, though, with the drab, square car park full of people milling around and chatting rather than just getting the hell away from the place — some were talking in hushed, slightly shocked tones; others had their TTCs attached to their ears and were frantically calling someone to determine *whether they'd heard the news.*

Stupid in itself, because whenever there was a piece of news deemed this important, every screen in the country automatically clocked over to the 'breaking news' setting. That way, no one was ever let out of the loop.

'Corin,' a voice called, and I shifted my position on the car to glare at the perpetrator. 'Corin, wait up!' Apparently my glare didn't quite convey as much hatred as intended, because Tom was still coming closer towards me, looking slightly wary but nevertheless determined.

'What?' I demanded, pushing myself back onto my feet and facing him.

'Mr Track told me to tell you,' he began, before I could make him leave by all means necessary, 'that Jacinta's been taken to the hospital. Just precautionary but, well, he said . . . to let you know.'

'Right,' I said, folding my arms and glaring at him. 'Did he also tell you where she left the goddamn house keys before she went gallivanting off to the psych ward? And did Mr Track give you details of my alternative travel arrangements?' A significant number of the people in the car park were looking at us now.

I turned away from Tom, who was standing with that slightly awkward posture of his when he didn't know quite what to say: a slack, lacklustre expression that had always grated on my nerves. I could understand that he didn't know what to do with what I'd given him, but that didn't excuse the dopey, vacant look either – he could at least be stony and unmoved.

Kicking the front door at exactly the right point always, inexplicably, clicked out the lock on the driver's side of the car so that the door swung open. That hardly helped when my thumb had been deleted from the identification archive. I pressed my useless thumb against the recognition pad anyway, hoping that somehow my mother had got wind of the situation and had decided to take pity on her poor abandoned daughter.

The 'error' message flashed on the screen of the sat nav. I kicked the car to vent my frustration with the whole day and tried again, as if my fingerprint would have shifted somehow in the last thirty seconds.

'Corin,' Tom said again, still behind me, 'look, it's my fault you can't drive your car – I'll give you a lift to the hospital.'

Claiming responsibility wasn't usually an activity Tom partook in. Obviously he was feeling guilty. Good.

'No.'

'Come on,' Tom said, reaching out and touching my arm. I pulled it out of his grasp and glared at him indignantly. 'Let me just drive you to the hospital.'

'I'd rather take the bus. I'd rather walk. I'd rather attach myself to the wheel of someone else's car and be continually run over all the way to the damn hospital.' Given the fact that the volume of my voice was just shy of yelling, it wasn't surprising that this rant was attracting a lot of attention. 'I'd rather camp here all night. I'd rather never get home. Actually, let's just save us both some bloody time – I would rather do *anything* than get in your car. OK? So why don't you find your soul mate and offer *him* a sodding lift!'

The *him* was a stroke of genius, inspired by Josaphine's gay father. Of course, loads of people were gay, and those people usually ended up in anima-vinculum friendships with a lover or two on the side (although that lifestyle wasn't exclusive to gay couples; some soul-mate bonding was just beyond sexual or romantic appearance, apparently). There were, however, only a few cases worldwide of same sex carpinomens and that was definitively a taboo.

In short, I was a damn genius.

Tom flushed slightly and took a step backwards. It struck me as ironic that this was probably the closest he was ever going to get to knowing that little more about me.

'You—' Tom began, expression twisting.

'Save it and sod off.'

'But—'

'I said, leave it.'

My thumb was shaking slightly as I forced it against the recognition pad. Again, a rejection and an error notice. Closing my eyes for a second, I realized that I needed to stop pretending so much — I almost felt like Tom had hurt me in some way and that I was angry at him. It was one thing convincing the world something was true, but it was bad when I started to believe it in my bones. There was enough deception going on these days without adding my own mind to the list of those not to be trusted.

'Need a lift?'

I looked up suddenly and found myself face to face with Colton Furnish.

'I'm fine.'

'I don't think your car's recognizing your fingerprints, actually.'

'Really?' I asked sarcastically, glaring up at him. 'I hadn't noticed.'

'Thought not, otherwise you would have accepted my lift,' Colton said with an easy smile. 'I'm going that way, anyway.'

'Need your eyes tested?' I suggested, jabbing the start button and vaguely hoping for a miracle. He raised his eyebrows at that. 'You obviously can't see that I'm *not* a damsel in distress.'

'Oh, right. So you're not stuck in the school car park until tomorrow morning without house keys or a mode of transport?'

'No,' I said, 'I'm not.'

'Stop being resentful and get in my car, Corin,' Colton said with a shrug of his shoulders. 'You're not going to get a better offer.'

'It's not a bleeding auction,' I conceded, shutting the car door with an overly forceful shove. 'I suppose your car can't be much worse than mine.'

'Mine doesn't open if you kick it,' Colton agreed, 'so I should think that's an improvement.'

'It is until you've lost your keys.'

Colton's car turned out to be much nicer than mine. I climbed into the front seat feeling slightly aware that people were still watching me before deciding that I couldn't care less. The car still had the lingering new-leather smell and an array of inviting buttons with complicated functions. No redundant gearstick, either.

'Going to admit you like it?'

'Wouldn't count on it,' I returned in a mumble. 'Let's get this on the road, Colt. The sooner you start driving the sooner it'll be over.'

'Right.' Colton grinned. 'Bitter Corin.'

'I've had a *really* bad day.'

'Yeah,' Colton agreed, glancing at me as he placed his thumb on the recognition pad and the engine kicked into life. 'I'll bet.' He was silent for a few minutes as we pulled out of the car park and onto the main road leading towards town. I relaxed on the seat slightly – the worst thing about getting a lift with someone you didn't know very well was them insisting on making conversation. If he'd added 'I'll be silent' to the end of his plea I wouldn't have bothered disagreeing in the first place. 'Is your sister OK?' he said now.

'She's fine,' I spat in annoyance, turning my back to look out the window. 'Just because she bloodied up her own wrists once, every time something like this happens on television they offer her a bed in the psych ward.'

The whole school knew the reason my sister had disappeared from school for a month when she was seventeen, why her boyfriend and his family uprooted and moved to a different continent and why, if someone slit their wrists in the D'livere, I might be a little on edge.

Colton wasn't expecting me to reference it, though – that was clear – and had instead expected some euphemistic talk surrounding the subject. Well, sod that. I hated the way my mother skirted around the issue as if not speaking the words plainly somehow diluted the reality behind them. It didn't. Maybe talking in such a frank manner made other people and the guidance councillors who assessed whether I was ready to be streamed uncomfortable, but it helped me. It was my family, my issue, my personal life – I should be allowed to talk about it how I wanted.

'She tried to kill herself.'

'No,' I countered, 'she didn't. She just tried to slice off her carpinomen. It's not her fault it happened to be on her wrist, now, is it?'

'That's ridiculous.'

'You're right about that,' I agreed, clamming up and staring resolutely out the window.

'I wasn't meaning her,' Colton said. His gaze from the mirror itched into the back of my neck. 'I'm in your O&E class.'

'I know,' I deadpanned. 'You're on top, I'm at the bottom – we established this a couple of hours ago, Colt. I'm not the one with mental problems.'

'Well,' Colton returned, 'I didn't think I'd ever shown up on your radar.'

'Flashing red light, all alarms buzzing. I don't get in the car with total strangers, you know.'

'You got in a car with Tom Asquith,' Colton pointed out. I turned round to face him at that. He was relaxation personified with his fingers tapping lightly against the steering wheel, shoulders sloped at an easy angle, dark hair hanging over his face – except his eyes, which were fixed a little too exactly on the road.

'If that's a euphemism, I want you to stop the car right now.'

'It wasn't,' Colton said with a grin. 'I liked what you did there, by the way – his face was great when you threw out that *him* curveball.'

'I like curveballs.' I shrugged slightly.

'Quite a show in general, actually,' Colton continued, eyes still fixed on the road. 'Almost believed the jilted act for a second.'

'Act?' I asked slowly. 'Why would I pretend to be upset?'

'I haven't worked that bit out yet,' Colton said. His fingers stopped tapping the steering wheel and instead curved around its surface. God knows why, but he was nervous. Given the direction the conversation seemed to be heading, I was the one who needed to be nervous. 'At first I thought you might just be a bit stupid. You haven't been streamed up to FE, after all, but then you've got the highest marks in O&E. Did you know Thomas is the most common name in the European and American Section?'

'Your point?'

'It's just, Corin, there is a slight difference between Tom and Thomas. And T-O-M-A-S Tomas too, for that matter. So, as a girl with more than a couple of brain cells, you'd know that. So if you genuinely thought T-O-M-A-S Tomas, or T-H-O-M-A-S Thomas, was your soul mate then you'd have known that T-O-M Tom was not.'

'This isn't a spelling test,' I muttered.

'You'd also have known that the name on Tom's wrist was

not going to be Corin. So you framed him to make him look like a heartless bastard.'

'Are you going somewhere with this?'

'So I'd hazard a tentative guess that your carpinomen isn't a variation of Thomas at all. You picked that name and decided to convince everyone it was your carpinomen while working your way through all the Toms and Thomases the Education Centre has to offer.'

'There's a Thomas Ingleton in the cuisine stream,' I pointed out.

'If I were him, I'd be quaking in my chef hat.'

'History teacher called Thomus Davey.'

'If I were him, I'd be desperately holding onto my job.'

'I'm making a point, Colt, that there are plenty of Thomases I haven't gone near,' I said, turning in my seat to face him with a slight frown.

'The fact that you're aware of all these different Thomases ruins your point, Corin.'

'I have a good people memory,' I said pointedly, folding my arms over my chest and watching him carefully – I had to admit, despite my best intentions, Colton had managed to pique my interest slightly.

'OK,' he said, leaning forward to get a good look at a particularly awkward junction, 'what do you know about me?'

'Your parents have a very common taste in names,' I said. 'You're my age, were streamed into non-specific further education around five months ago, started taking O&E classes two months ago and are reasonably talented at it, have been in Tom Asquith's car, apparently like to overthink things and butt into people's personal lives, are desperately lonely and will do anything to provoke conversation. Pass your test?'

'Not even close.' Colton grinned. 'Been at school together since we were four and that's all you know?'

'You weren't in many of my classes,' I said pointedly, 'and, frankly, before this conversation you never struck me as particularly interesting. What does it matter to you whether I'm heartbroken or not?'

'Tom Asquith is a good guy.' Colton shrugged. 'Didn't deserve to have his name dragged through the mud.'

'Bonded over your stupidly common names, did you?'

'I rode with him in the last ration week,' Colton supplied. 'He thinks rather a lot of you, considering how heartlessly you disposed of him.'

'Considering you're approaching this from a moral angle, you seem a little too impressed,' I said distractedly, glancing at the road signs and feeling relieved that we were nearly there.

'Admirer of literature and drama in all mediums.' He shrugged. 'Shame there's no stream for that.'

I gave Colton a mental thumbs up for that. The amount of literature and drama in the public domain was very little and very underappreciated. Usually when I confessed to a love of books and reading I was greeted with a disturbed raise of the eyebrows. The whole world was obsessed with the science we used to half destroy the planet, rather than the few things of beauty we still had left. Anyone with a *genuine* love of literature instantly went up in my estimation.

'A modern-day tragedy,' I added dryly. 'So, I played Tom for a fool. You planning on telling the world?'

'Wouldn't count on it,' Colton said, pulling into the hospital car park, 'if you promise to tell me why.'

'Unlikely.'

'Stalemate, then,' Colton said as he pushed his car door open and began climbing out. 'I'll get back to you.'

'Wait,' I said, following him. 'You're not coming with me to the hospital.'

'Yes I am,' Colton countered, locking the car door behind him and walking up to the hospital with me hurrying two steps behind him. A deep-rooted panic seemed to have started to ache in my gut: the idea of Colton, or anyone, actually, seeing my sister when she might be at her most vulnerable was horrible. Admittedly there wasn't actually anything wrong with Jacinta but a tendency to seek attention, because she was no more likely to take another knife to her wrist than I was. Letting them admit her to hospital every time something like this happened just gave her an intermittent refuge away from real life. Who wouldn't want to spend a couple of days unmarred by the pressure of the world? Who wouldn't want to spend a few days buzzed up on some concoction of drugs? Who wouldn't give anything just to be allowed not to think for a few minutes, and just to exist as a functioning body rather than a whole human being? That's what the psych ward gave Jacinta whenever she played the right cards — and that was the real insanity of the situation.

But I still didn't want anyone to see her drugged up, wired

up to a couple of machines and one surveillance level down from suicide watch.

'I'd rather you told the world that Thomas isn't my carpinomen than visit my goddamn sister,' I said, grabbing hold of his arm and forcing him to stop. 'I don't care what your reasoning is – I'll be five minutes, if that, and if you could just wait . . . and if you don't want to do that then I'll just wait here for my mum, but you're not—'

'Relax, Corin,' Colton said with a slight smile.

'Let me guess, you've only seen a hospital once and you want to explore? Well—'

'My parents are doctors,' Colton interrupted, 'my baby sister is in the crèche and I needed to come here to pick her up. Don't get excited, Corin, I really meant I was coming this way.'

I took a deep breath while simultaneously trying to ensure that I didn't look like I was taking a deep breath. I could hardly believe that just twenty minutes ago I'd been suggesting that I was acting too much, when now here was Colton Furnish who somehow knew that I'd been placing a false carpinomen trail and, worse, knew that the idea of him seeing my sick sister made me nervous.

'Are you OK?' Colton asked with a slight drawl. God, he was arrogant. The worst kind of arrogant too – the kind of arrogant that knows and accepts its own arrogance because it stems from some secret moral code. So he thought he had a right to look at me and judge me because he reckoned he could see all my thoughts and had an idea of how he'd have done things differently.

People like that know nothing.

'Fine,' I said lightly, shoving my hands into the pockets of my trousers and taking another step towards the building.

The hospital was ugly and very square, but that seemed to be the architectural flavour of the month when they were rebuilding the city out of the rusty, metal age of waste. Now buildings were fashioned to almost be self-sustainable. The science was probably available for complete sustainability, but then we wouldn't need a government, and politicians would never let that happen.

'Sure? Because if you need an escort, I could probably show you around.'

'You act like I don't know my way around a psych ward,' I quipped back with a light smile — all these years of stupid boyfriends who wanted stupid girls who could flirt and smile and simper had paid off, as I'd always suspected they would. Jacinta wasn't the only one with a number of default settings.

'Corin Blacksmith,' Colton grinned, nodding his head towards me in a mock token of respect, 'I'd never assume such a thing.'

4

Issues of Sanity

There was a series of family photos in our corridor at home, most of them pre-dating the things that tore apart reality by a year or so, and I always found it surprising that I actually liked them.

It wasn't entirely a mark of sentimentality, because I rarely allowed myself to sit and dwell on the years before Dad died or when Jacinta was in the psych ward. Dwelling on things wasn't as shocking and heart-wrenching as much as irritating, because those years had passed by and that was that. It sucked, really it did, but it wasn't like staring dreamily at a photo of my dad's receding hairline was going to bring him back to life, and willing Jacinta into being *OK* hadn't worked for my mother thus far — for all her hoping, all she perpetuated was disappointment. It wasn't worth it.

I liked one photo in particular because it seemed to capture so much of our personality as a family and I found it interesting that one moment frozen in time could tell you so much.

Neither Jacinta nor I were particularly cute children — it was strange to see my large masculine nose, my wide blue-grey eyes and my pointed chin on the face of a child.

My mother was right when she described my appearance as aggressive. I always thought that she meant it as a criticism, but I liked everything about the idea of it. I played up to it and cut my hair into a brutal fringe across my face using a ruler and a pair of scissors. Anorexic eyebrows, lips full to bursting point, pale blonde hair that awkward length that everyone tries to avoid — just past jaw-length.

I'd grown into it, but as a child there were too many features fighting to dominate my face. In the picture my hair is longer but just as straight, hanging where my breasts would be if the photo hadn't pre-dated that, and I am not smiling. It was an inquisitive *What's going on?* expression that Mum later labelled as my trademark.

Jacinta sits next to me in the photograph. That was always strange to see, because now we try to distance ourselves from each other as much as possible. Jacinta's hair is a shade darker, her features slightly less extreme, and her smile softens her own slightly crooked nose and too-sharp chin to the point where they seem almost unremarkable. The smile is, however, pinned onto her face out of the will of our parents — you can see from her eyes that she isn't happy either.

The truth of that lurks behind us, where Mum and Dad stand. Dad's hand lightly touches Mum's shoulder, in a way which seems too considered and designed for me to believe it (this was probably because I knew it, not through the actual detail of the photo) and Mum's shoulder tenses beneath his touch — they are both entirely on edge, all their limbs at purposeful angles and all their expressions carefully designed for the sake of playing *happy families*.

Jacinta and I are too far away from them. We have distanced ourselves from their pretence.

The portrait reminds me that as soul mates go, Mum and Dad were both rubbish at keeping their relationship problems from us, and in response Jacinta and I kept our own secrets. Our family was a long messy game of scoring points against each other.

Then Dad died, and now Jacinta and I are the only two still playing. It used to be that we would try to play for attention. Jacinta was a genius and I was perceptive beyond my years. Now, that sort of thing barely penetrates our mother's skull, so I stay out late with guys and Jacinta keeps ending up back in the psych ward.

And all the damn time, none of us are telling each other the truth.

It was safer.

'I was hoping you'd be unconscious,' I told Jacinta as I stepped towards her bed. The med staff recognized me, so let me visit without signing the usual forms, brushing off my sarcastic comments as usual and being quite accommodating and helpful. It was easy enough to see why Jacinta liked to spend time here.

'Same,' Jacinta retorted, her voice softened slightly by whatever meds she'd gladly shoved down her throat. She didn't need them. She didn't need *this*.

'Could have given me the damn keys before you got yourself sectioned.'

I took another step towards her, kicked the visitor's seat from off the wall and sat down on it heavily.

'Don't be ignorant, Corin,' Jacinta returned. 'I haven't been bloody sectioned.'

'Not this time.'

'Sod off.'

'Gladly. I only came for the house keys.'

'I haven't got them,' Jacinta said lightly, closing her eyes. 'They were removed from my person.'

'God's sake,' I grunted, 'do you have to be so damn selfish?'

'Careful, they'll chuck you out again, Corin.'

'That would be interesting,' I said, smiling slightly. 'Colton Furnish gave me a lift here — I'd like to see how he'd react to me explaining I'd been kicked out of the psych ward. How do I get the keys?'

'You need to talk to one of the nurses,' Jacinta said. 'They're only keeping me in overnight.'

'As there's absolutely nothing wrong with you.'

Jacinta sat up. In hospital, her movements were looser and freer and much more spontaneous than usual; so much so that her sudden jerk into movement startled me slightly.

She reached for her bedside table and unscrewed the cap on the prescription drugs that were making her so amiable and, well, almost *normal*.

'I'm in control of my own meds,' Jacinta said by way of explanation.

'Poor decision on the medical staff's behalf.'

'Want one?' Jacinta questioned, glancing up to make sure none of the nurses were in the near vicinity. She tipped one of the pills onto her hand and held it out to me. 'Sisters share, after all,' she added, with her old upbeat sarcasm dripping into her words.

'What's your dosage?'

'Three,' Jacinta said, tipping another few pills onto her palm.

I took two. Swallowed one without water and considered the other one. 'Why?'

'Like I said, they're only going to keep me in overnight.'

'So you're fake overdosing,' I returned, shaking my head slightly as I took the second. 'Nice.'

'Not want the third?' Jacinta prompted. I shook my head. 'Don't think you're as crazy as me, then?'

'Neither of us are crazy,' I said, pulling myself up out of my seat before the pills could have any effect. God knows what they'd do, but I didn't feel like facing the nurses if I'd been drugged up by something. The things I did for my sister. 'Try and stay the week, why don't you? I could do with some peace and quiet.'

'I'll aim to.'

'Thanks,' I said, pulling back the curtain and setting about trying to find a nurse. I didn't much like hospitals. Definitely didn't think much of my sister. But, on the whole, the pills weren't all that bad.

They hadn't done anything really, but having the autonomy to self-destruct was nice.

'You seem to have a lack of baby sister, Colt,' I commented on reaching the car, gripping hold of the handle on the car door slightly to make sure I was absolutely fine on the standing-up front. My head was spinning slightly. I was beginning to think that I should have asked Jacinta what the bloody meds were actually for.

'Mum's sick and took her home after lunch,' Colton said with a shrug of his shoulders, watching me in that slightly too-careful way of his. 'How's Jacinta?'

'As ridiculous as always,' I returned, yanking open the car door and sitting down heavily in the passenger seat. 'Had to wrestle a nurse to get the keys. Then I got a lecture on being supportive, or something.'

'Being supportive?' Colton suggested. 'The nurse hadn't met you before, then?'

I swore at him.

Colton laughed and shook his head, turning the car on and heading out towards the entrance of the car park. 'My dad works on your sister's ward,' he continued in a conversational manner which was definitely inappropriate for the subject he was broaching. 'Said it was only an overnight stop.'

'Doubt it,' I muttered, pressing a hand to my forehead and concluding that Jacinta's pills were the work of the devil. If I could just close my eyes and let the world spin then it wouldn't be so bad, but being forced into conversation and seeing everything so clearly and brightly and just . . . 'Jacinta's got her own priorities and they don't involve being kind to the hospital resources,' I added.

'Or you?' Colton suggested. I sent him a dark look. 'Look, Corin, you have a point – she could have left your keys with reception, or Tom, or one of your other friends.'

'Right,' I said, 'because Jacinta knows who my friends are.'

'See?' Colton said. 'You don't exactly speak highly of her.'

'And that's my prerogative. You don't know much about siblings, Colt.' I frowned slightly. The car seemed to be going awfully quick to me. 'Do you know where I live?'

'Street down from me. I see you driving to school. Which is strange, considering your car doesn't recognize your fingerprints?'

'Unladylike conduct got me taken off the insurance,' I admitted. 'Jacinta ratted me out to Mother, Mother got angry, Corin can't drive. Except Jacinta hates driving, so I *can* drive as long as she's there. Hopefully they'll put her back on her meds and then Mum'll have to let up.'

'Are you OK?'

'Perfectly.'

'You look a bit . . .' Colton paused, glancing over in my direction with a slightly odd expression.

'Eyes on the road.'

'Are you drunk?'

'Oh, you've got it. It must be all this *alcohol* you've seen me drinking.'

Colton was silent for a few minutes. 'Drugged?'

'I asked for a lift, not an interrogation,' I said pointedly. 'You convince me to get in your car and then you start asking some really quite personal questions. I'm not wearing a badge that says "get to know me". I pride myself on giving out pretty negative vibes, so, Colton Furnish, why the hell do you think you can start asking me about my carpinomen or my ex-boyfriends?'

'I'm pulling over,' Colton said. 'You're obviously insane.'

'Wrong sister.'

'You bet I've got the right one,' Colton said, turning left into the centre of the village and pulling over to the side of the road, outside a café. 'You're not all right, Corin. And I want to know what sort of state you're in before I drive off.'

'I'm fine.'

'Great — what did you take?'

'What would it take to make you sod off?'

'Yeah, I get it, you're a witty genius. Now, come on, what's the deal?'

'What's it to you?'

'You're in my car, that's what. If you're about to start throwing up or having a fit or something I'd like to know what I'm dealing with,' Colton said, his voice rising in volume slightly.

'I'm not going to have a fit,' I countered, my fingers curling over the edge of the seat belt as I blinked. I did feel better now we weren't moving. 'Jacinta wanted me to take some of her meds.'

'Why?'

'So she can stay in the bloody hospital!' I said. 'And now my head's spinning and I'm apparently more forward with information. It's not a big deal, Colton, and if you tell your dad I'll be arrested for stealing from the hospital so, that's great, now you have the power to get me thrown in prison and also sent to a loony bin for creating a false carpinomen trail. Congratulations, you've ruined my life.'

'So you admit your carpinomen isn't Tom, then?' Colton asked. I kept my mouth firmly shut. 'Let's get coffee,' he said, unlocking the car and pushing the door open.

I followed him out again, feeling stupid. Now it was my movements that were more spontaneous and slightly too erratic. Should have just taken the one pill and smuggled the other out in my shoe or something, or just said no to Jacinta's offer. Then again, if I hadn't taken the pill, *she* would have, and the last thing Mum needed was a *genuine* overdose.

'Why?'

'You can't go home like that,' Colton said pointedly. 'I mean, I don't think it's that obvious, but if your mum's seen Jacinta on her meds it's not like she wouldn't notice.'

'Are you streamed in logic?'

'No.' Colton grinned. 'Non-specific, we established that.'

'Whatever,' I conceded, grabbing hold of his arm to keep myself upright.

Colton raised his eyebrows, looked at me and offered a ridiculously smug smirk. I couldn't even care less, at this point — I wasn't some giggling pre-bonded girl who went jittery thanks to touching someone's arm. Mostly that was the calibre of girls my age — for most people, the first person they ever kissed was their soul mate. It wasn't frowned upon to date early on, when you were about fifteen, but after that you were supposed to save yourself for the search and your carpinomen.

Like I said, I'm not very good at following rules.

'So,' Colton said, pushing open the door of the café for me and holding it open with another smirk, 'let's talk about your sister.'

'No,' I said, taking a seat near the door, 'let's not. I'll have a double espresso, please.'

'I'm getting you a cup of tea,' Colton said. 'Last thing you need is more strong stimulant, if it *is* a stimulant. I suppose you didn't read the label before swallowing it? No? Maybe I am revaluating my "isn't stupid" comment from earlier.'

'A moment of spontaneous idiocy doesn't equate to being stupid.'

'Just being an idiot.'

'Precisely,' I agreed, folding my legs in the chair and pulling out my TTC. The homepage, government-selected, was still alive with the buzz of the death in the D'livere, and I scrolled through several media icons' opinions: sometimes I had to remind myself that Britain still prided itself on its free press; it was just that fame and lots of money was the price of it — as long as you were rich, you were allowed to have an opinion.

'Sending angry texts to the ex-boyfriend?' Colton suggested, sitting down again after going up to order. 'I hear you shouldn't contact the ex when dosed up on illicit substances.'

'What would you know?' I asked pointedly. 'Saving your-self for the one?'

'Or just someone.'

I could almost hear that unvoiced 'not just anyone' and the tone of accusation that would accompany it. Great; even Colton thought I was a slut. I'd add him to the mental list.

'You don't know anything about me.'

'No one does,' Colton said, leaning forward. The almost dramatic moment was cut off by the waitress arriving with our tea. It was an added knife in the gut when I realized that this was Amy from O&E class, who would no doubt spend recreational time tomorrow telling her friends all about how she saw Colton Furnish and Corin Blacksmith on a date in a coffee shop. 'Except everyone thinks they do.'

'Enlightening,' I said dryly. 'What does everyone think about me, then?'

'That your carpinomen is Thomas, for one. Damaged emotionally. Attachment issues.'

'And I'm the one on drugs here? Look, Colt, you might be stalking me, but most of the world really doesn't care what the hell I'm doing. Still, certainly didn't expect to end the day on a date with you.'

'A date?' Colton questioned, his expression freezing slightly. 'This isn't a date.'

'Boy, girl, coffee, you trying to get to know me; sounds like a date to me.'

'A date would involve me saying, "Corin, let's go on a date."'

'You said, "Let's go get coffee." I was filling in the subtext.'

'Don't,' Colton advised. 'Could get you in a dangerous position one day.'

'Why don't we keep this pedestrian?' I suggested, leaning forward in my seat and smiling at him slightly — people like Colt were too easy to manipulate because they were crude and obvious and had too much faith in the world.

'Pedestrian?' Colt repeated.

'Impersonal, standard, phatic talk; we could talk about the weather.'

'Right,' Colton said. 'Well, it's England. It's raining. I say we throw that idea to hell and you answer some of my questions.'

'Look, you can't ask me personal questions because I've taken some prescription drugs that were not prescribed to me, so I'm not quite as with it as usual. If you ask me personal questions, then you're taking advantage.' I paused, reached out and ran my finger over the edge of his wrist guard — *anima-praesido*, as the more romantic might call it — and let my finger hover just over the catch. 'The thing is, Colt, people who set out to take advantage of me usually end up in a much worse position than they started. So, even if your pretty moral code isn't enough to stop you probing, please try to remember that I'm a bitch and I *really* don't care about any aspect of your life.'

For a second I considered just walking out, but he hadn't *really* done anything wrong but show an interest and, anyway, his car was the only way home. I chose to take another delicate sip of my tea instead.

Colton leaned back in his chair, taking a gulp of his own

tea with an unfathomable expression, before his lips twisted into an almost impressed smile. Then his face softened and took on the sort of appearance one might use when trying to encourage a small child.

God, it was annoying.

'And thanks for the tea,' I finished, with my own sweet smile in return.

The alarming effects of the drugs had worn off by the time Colton dropped me off at home, leaving me feeling slightly more relaxed than normal.

Honestly, I didn't like it; Jacinta might like the release from responsibilities and the lack of tension, but I prefer to end each day with my shoulder muscles rock-hard from keeping them clenched all day. Plus, it was difficult to focus on the whole host of issues that the day had upturned: for one, Colton had managed to advance from being some random guy who lived quite close to me to being someone who held actual power over me — and it did nothing to quench my dulled nervousness (if I hadn't been drugged up, I'd have surely developed a tension headache by now) that he'd left with the promise to pick me up for school tomorrow because: *'Isn't that what people do after a nice date, Corin? Make plans to see each other again?'* He'd only come up with the date line when I'd proposed a *goodbye kiss* which had, disturbingly, made him laugh.

The worst part of it all was that I genuinely felt like I hadn't spent the hour or so in his company acting; I'd probably been more myself, drugged up or not, than I had been with anyone for a long time. It seemed I'd saturated my acting ability by spending the whole day playing out various degrees of distress about Tom Asquith so that I just *physically* couldn't do it any longer.

More important was the death in the D'livere. Ignoring the effect it would have on my own life — because, really, most of the time it was a lot easier to ignore Jacinta than it was to pay any attention to her — it was another politically motivated act of defiance.

There had been a few politically motivated suicides lately. Four months ago, the son of the Minister for Justice for the entire European Section had killed himself on an old war memorial. Broken in, somehow, so he must have had help from at least half a dozen other conspirators, draped himself over the white marble of one of the unmarked graves, taken his wrist guard off and slit his wrists; they didn't show the pictures on the news, but it wasn't the blood or even his exposed wrists that they thought would make the general public feel uncomfortable — the poor sod had written his name and the name of his soul mate with the blood pouring from his wrists, so that *Ronan and Keara* shone just below the time-old inscription *Known unto God* in a fantastical, brutal, bloody red.

Just thirty miles from that graveyard and six weeks later, this 'Keara' had shown up — there was a media frenzy trying to find her up until that point, holding onto some desperate hope that they could still play the suicide off as a love story, rather than an act of rebellion. No such luck. Keara was filmed hammering a diamond-crusted nail through her boyfriend's wrist guard as he read out an extract from the Bible. The voluntary crucifixion was one of the most horrific videos I'd ever watched and the vulgarity of the thing was increased by the note that came encrypted with the file — they could have saved his life, if the doctors had been prepared to take off his wrist guard. They had hesitated a few seconds too long and that was it — a nameless boy in love with a girl who was not his soul mate joined the ranks of the dead.

That aspect of the story hadn't been reported in the news at all and I'd been hard-pressed to persuade my contact even to send me the video, although that was more out of fear of my delicate stomach than confidentiality.

I'd since tried tracing Keara's fate, but my contact had nothing to offer. She was probably in prison, or receiving mandatory psychiatric help. It was difficult to be sure.

There'd been other deaths too, leading up to the most notable case so far, but there were always similarities: they were all young and had recently started their search, their soul mates were always involved and it was always the wrists. There was something pseudo-romantic, it seemed, about hacking into the place where your soul was laid bare for the world to see, and using it as a marker — 'cut here' — or a self-destruct button that needed to be activated.

I plugged my TTC into my full tabloid screen and it burst into light.

It took half an hour of typed flirting to achieve my aim — although I'd gone a tad overboard thanks to my ever so slightly addled brain — and to begin downloading the full security tape from the D'livere this afternoon.

The version my contact had sent through wasn't as blurry as the version shown on the television, but the video quality still left something to be desired. I leaned back to get the full view of the scene.

The two walked into the D'livere, side by side. Her face had been shown on the news bulletin and I suspected that it would be almost everywhere for the next few weeks. Soon, I'd be sick of seeing her face . . . now, it was an intriguing symbol of some cause I'd yet to grasp. What was she trying to achieve? What was the point?

After a few seconds she exchanged a look with him, he crossed the dome to the security guard and started asking a question. The volume was muffled too, but I could just about make out the fact that he was challenging the obvious — angrily stating that he thought the government was lying about no one ever dying in the D'livere, that there was no possible way the government could prove that sort of claim, and teetering on the edge of accusing the security guard of fascism. I was so enthralled by his rhetoric that I almost missed the moment.

I skipped back a few seconds and watched her slip the knife out of her wrist guard. It was small and unassuming; it wasn't the sort of weapon you expected to bring the world to its knees, yet it inevitably had. She didn't remove her wrist guard and instead pushed it up her arm — she must have lost a lot of weight to be able to do that, which meant that the whole event had to have been planned for weeks. Months, even. The whole point of wrist guards was that they couldn't slip off — they were a permanent handcuff protecting your carpinomen from being compromised.

There was, after all, logic behind that *don't tell anyone the name on your wrist* rule — to stop others from being able to rip away what was most important to you.

She was wearing a blood-red jumper too. She pulled her sleeves over her wrists and wrapped them in the edge of her jumper to stop the blood dripping to the floor so obviously. She was a sickly pale colour before the security guard noticed, and that was when her companion threw his arms out wide and started yelling. He wouldn't let anyone get to her. She fell. The other tourists pressed themselves against the edge of the Perspex dome and tried to back away, unconsciously hindering the security guard by getting in his way. When the guy could not hold the guard off any longer, he sank to the ground next to the dying girl and wrapped his body around her as she bled out.

He kept saying the same damn thing, over and over, as the security guard tried to lift the pair of them the hell out of there, before he realized that it was simply too late.

There were bloody marks and handprints at the edge of the D'livere, the Perspex tainted by bloodied prints. Death, it seemed, was always going to win.

And the guy kept saying, '*She's my soul mate and I'm glad she wanted to die because I hate her.*'

I saved the video in the file with the rest, flicked over to some mundane makeover programme and settled down to watch it in bed.

I suspected I'd be asleep before they got a significant way

into the girl's incredible transformation, but it was something safe to leave on for when my mum returned home to assure her that I was just fine.

It was Jacinta she had to worry about.

Probably.

5

The Downfall of Jacinta Blacksmith

Jacinta looked to be in a state even closer to Hell than usual, which was pretty scary considering that in about three minutes' time Colton was going to arrive to pick us up. He'd been giving me a lift for three weeks now, but this was the first time he'd meet my sister.

This was why I hated ration week. I mean, sure, I knew that these things were necessary to keep up the standard of living: instead of continually forcing the message of reducing electrical usage down our throats, the government initiative was for each area, county or city to have a regular week of 'rationing' where electricity and petrol were only used where absolutely essential. All those who commuted or travelled to work had to either sign up for the bus, which was guaranteed to stop within a three-minute walking distance of your front door but usually just didn't run, state their intention to travel by train, or sign up to a car pool with a designated driver and five full seats (or more, if you had them). For all other cars, their recognition pads were blocked for all but those who worked in the emergency services – who could start any car at will, anyway. Tabloids were powered off for an entire week, with the only function left being that they could still charge the TTC sections of the machine. Each house was given a limited supply of electricity – if you wanted to turn all the lights on at the same time, then you might not have enough power to cook dinner. Not using all your electrical credits could lead to a financial reward, if you were the best, and running out early usually resulted in begging neighbours for the use of their hot shower.

It was played up to be a sort of game. When we were younger we'd had to attend compulsory history lessons about rations and war and how those before us had all but ruined the planet – and why now there's a two-child rule and why we don't mine for coal any more. All fascinating stuff when you're five years old and still believe it, but I know for a fact that most countries are still operating underground oil rigs due to the stats not working out any other way. There are at least three nuclear power stations hidden somewhere in the country, and although the horrors of cancer are more or less a thing of the past, public opinion is still very much against nuclear in any form – so, officially, these don't exist.

Of course, being a pre-streamed teenager it's not like I had anything to support this theory. They might, for example, be much better at producing renewable electricity than the government let on, but considering how much money the government paid people to ensure they looked decent, it was unlikely. Humanity is just so very good at boasting about the things they are supposedly good at, and hushing up the things they don't want anyone else to know.

On a personal level, what all the politics of electricity and ration and excess meant was that, every so often, I had to arrange transport for Jacinta. And it was crap.

She was usually too disinclined to sort something else for herself and it was always more difficult to find room in a car for two. Eventually I'd given up and settled on the prospect of the bus (as detestable as it was, some of those things actually still *needed* a gearstick), unless of course ration week collided with a period of Thomas – then after a bit of manipulation and pouting from me it was virtually their duty to ensure that both Jacinta and I were accounted for.

Then, after I was signing up for the use of the bus with the other losers and eco-freaks, Colton had appeared out of nowhere, raised an eyebrow and calmly stated that he had two seats in his car that were still free.

Colton and I had developed an almost-friendship of sorts, whereby he'd nodded pointedly to the seat next to him in O&E classes, given me lifts the entire time Jacinta was in hospital (she managed nearly two weeks, in the end) and occasionally nagged me with personal questions that weren't actually so bad to answer. Categorically I didn't have friends, but I couldn't shake him off when his car was so very helpful to my life.

If only he'd said 'one' seat I could have heartlessly abandoned Jacinta, but he'd anticipated that I'd no doubt be willing to do that and might even feel bad about it later (over-generous on his behalf; I was far and beyond the stage when I still felt sorry for Jacinta Blacksmith). Either way, my knee-jerk reaction had been to eschew the bus with a very firm hand and, in doing so, had actually dragged Jacinta a little closer.

Bad position to be in, really.

'Do you act like yourself around him?' Jacinta asked, jerking up from her breakfast suddenly and staring at me sharply.

'Why, are you planning to? Because I don't think you've got enough drugs in your system for it.' I took a sip of my coffee with my lips slightly pursed. Most of the times I'd organized a lift for Jacinta, the lift-giver had a tendency to pretend that she wasn't there. Colton, however, was sure to try and spark up a conversation. The idea worried me slightly.

'I need to prepare myself for not reacting to whichever of your alter egos I'm reacquainted with,' Jacinta retorted, only there was an edge of actual interest in her voice. Oh dear, Jacinta *was* acting more like my sister than the robot that had taken her place years previously. And she was going to meet Colton.

'I thought you weren't interested in my life.'

'Not your sex life,' Jacinta said, glancing towards the door as if to reassure herself that our mother wasn't in. 'I wasn't aware that you were sleeping with him.'

'How would you know?' I asked, drinking a little more coffee.

'Oh, Corin,' Jacinta said, eyes narrowing. 'Everybody knows.'

'I hadn't realized you were engaged enough in reality to listen to idle gossip,' I spat back, standing up and taking away her plate before she'd quite finished her toast. 'I'd prefer it if you didn't talk.'

'I'm sure you would,' Jacinta said, standing up to her full height – and once again reminding me that she was taller – 'but we don't always get what we want, do we?'

I glanced down at her wrists deliberately.

'Evidently.'

That was horrible. Way beyond the realms of the things we usually said to each other, but I was feeling oddly vulnerable and, apparently, that led to me lashing out. I didn't know what Colton was going to say to my sister and, worse, I didn't know what Jacinta would say in response – I'd convinced myself that she'd fall into the usual robotic routine, which was fine, but she seemed too engaged with life this morning for that to be possible.

'Who else are we riding with?'

'Damien Elton and his kid sister,' I said, shoulders tensing slightly as I glanced at the door.

Colton had asked about my sister obsessively, and to absolute silence from my part. A lot of the facts were common knowledge and, as far as I was concerned, everyone could make a judgement themselves. Colton didn't need to know how the whole business had made me feel, or anything of that sort. It was done, the past, just one of those things.

Jacinta was seventeen when she ruined her life.

Later, her step into self-destruction would be put down to the grief of losing our father seeping through her skin and messing her up in some way, but I never bought that.

The thing about death is that it isn't the end for everyone else: people die and there's no handbook on how to deal with it, so you just have to carry on by all means necessary. Everyone grieves differently, feels differently — like my mother, for example. She didn't talk to either of us for a week and then continued as though nothing had happened. It was only years later that she stopped pretending that our father had never existed and began to speak in that nostalgic tone we'd all been expecting from day one. She never broke down — that was her own personal form of grief. She just got on with it because that was life and that was the way it was.

Sure, Jacinta was messed up . . . but only in the same way that every other teenager is messed up. It starts with the parents who love their child so much they make up stories and futures for them before they even exist, yet parents aren't always the best at fortune-telling and, because of that, they often form ideals about their child that are unrealistic and impossible to attain.

And that means you feel like you're not good enough. Everyone has a jigsaw outline carved out for them by their parents, and parents try and push you to fit in that frame, and you either squeeze yourself into a space you were never designed to fit or you snap and refuse to try — bend or break.

Neither stop your parents loving you, neither stop their slight resentment at you not being exactly what they wanted, and neither stop you loving your parents back.

Then the rest of the world joins in on the act — everyone is subjected to preconceptions and ideals of how you should be, how you should want to be, what you should do. Nothing screws up a person as much as others expecting things from them. The world lets you down, you get bent out of shape, you can't quite make the cut, or when you do it isn't exactly what you always dreamed it would be — everyone, after all, is broken and then fixed with sticky tape and bits of string.

And, yes, Jacinta was affected by that just as much as the next person. Much, much more, some might argue.

His name was Brett Jones. Just a teenager, really, nothing all that special — on the attractive side of normal, slightly older than Jacinta but not as clever and the instrument of all her ruin. I was closer to Jacinta at that point, but still not exactly on friend's terms. After all, I was her kid sister who always seemed to be getting into trouble and was generally a pain in her arse.

She was streamed into Further Education early, just before she was seventeen, and she was in his Further chemistry classes. They were talking about streaming her into the doctor training courses and him into the nurse training courses. A medical match made in heaven which, two weeks after they met, resulted in the two being positively in-separable.

I was oozing with jealousy. At fifteen I was adamant that I wanted to be soul-bonded more than anything in the world and it seemed like Jacinta had finally got there. I then produced my first Thomas (in the beginning, it was the desire for others to think that I too had found a soul mate; Level One O&E classes taught me that Thomas was the most popular name – hey presto), although that didn't stop me attempting to flirt with Brett. Pitiful attempts really, because I was fifteen and he was eighteen, so to him I was just a little kid and Jacinta found it irritating rather than the stab in the back I'd intended.

Then Jacinta started to go off the rails. She still spent as much time with Brett as ever, but she seemed to be drifting away from all her friends. Once she actually ended up in a fist fight with her old best mate, Davina, which I'd never have believed if I hadn't burst into her room unannounced and seen the crescent moon bruises on her shoulder from where Davina had dug her fingers into my sister's skin. The Education Centre started to ask questions about whether anything was going on at home and she was held back from her initial doctor training.

I remember the day when everything hit the fan as clearly as I remember anything. It's ingrained into my memory like a physical scar – it doesn't matter what happens to me, I won't ever be able to forget it.

Jacinta and Brett had skipped school, which wasn't uncommon in those days – no one said anything, as they believed that Jacinta and Brett were anima-vinculum and that, perhaps, he was the answer to sorting out her mixed-up, mashed-up emotions after Dad's death. Still, Jacinta had been in charge of driving the two of us to and from school since she turned sixteen and now I was abandoned at school with no way of getting home. Thomas — the first Thomas — gave me a lift home and I wasted a lot of time kissing him in the front of his car while my sister was sitting in the living room with a knife to her wrists.

After Thomas had driven off I saw the twisted metal remains that had been my sister's car — she'd driven into something, never found out what, and the nose had crumpled into a corrugated, mournful shape that still haunts me sometimes. Then I knew something was wrong.

I was torn between running into the house and never wanting to open the door. The fear was bubbling up in my gut, and making it impossible to move and impossible to stay still. It wasn't the first time I'd come home after Jacinta and expected to find the worst — normally a whole arsenal of images and scenarios flittered through my brain and clouded my vision and made my heart race. That day, though, my mind was utterly blank.

The house had never seemed so silent and deadly, my heart was thumping in my mouth, and every door I opened that revealed nothing was both a breath of release and a stab in the gut.

The living room was the fourth door I tried.

And she was there, and I thought she was dead because all I could smell was the stench of blood, and the sharp light reflected off the knife and bruised my retinas. Frozen in the doorway, I remember thinking, *Who's going to drive me to school?* before the ice thawed out and I fell into the room.

Jacinta looked up at me, her eyes clotted with tears that

had dried out while I was still in my last lesson, and her eye-lashes still sticking together because of them; her wrists were bare and naked and bloody.

I pulled the knife out of her hands and I put it on the table next to her. I ripped one of my shirts off the radiator and placed her bloody wrists on top of them. I called the hospital. I sat down next to her. All of this was done with a falsely calm state in my bones, without shaking, and I remember thinking, *The fact that they can see her wrists is going to make the doctors feel uncomfortable,* and, *I wish that I could put her wrist guard back on for her.*

I didn't look at the name on her wrist. I didn't want to and, anyway, the name was the epicentre of all the damage — there was nothing left but a wound to read, not a name.

It was when the ambulance arrived that I started to lose it: then, while they were pulling her onto a stretcher and try-ing to get her to move (all her limbs seemed to be unable to bend, as if rigor mortis had already seeped into them) and whispering things into her ears, that I started to yell at her. I have absolutely no idea what I screamed. I think I prob-ably called her selfish for a million reasons. I think I probably accused her of being a coward for trying to kill herself because, as they loaded her into the taxi, she sobbed, 'I wasn't . . . Corin, I wasn't trying to kill myself . . . I don't want to die, I just . . . I needed his name off my wrist.'

And then it all made so much bloody sense.

Brett wasn't her carpinomen, but a boy she'd fallen in love with. She must have told him, he left, she crashed the car, drove home and tried to slice away the one thing she thought was stopping her from being happy. I hated her for it, for doing something so goddamn stupid – she must have known the relationship would end up in the gutter, must have realized that there was no way she could lie for ever. She should have thought about that before she let herself fall.

But then, who was I to talk? I was dating a guy called Thomas, when my carpinomen was something completely different altogether. I slept with him to prove that he meant nothing to me, got dumped for my efforts and decided that the whole world had to believe 'Thomas' was my carpinomen, or else they'd think me just as stupid as Jacinta.

And that really would be a tragedy.

Brett Jones's whole family moved away. My sister rotted in hospital for weeks. I moved the hell on – that's life, really.

There was no story there that Colton couldn't piece together, the same as I had done, and I didn't appreciate him bringing up all those inconvenient little memories.

'He's here,' Jacinta said. 'Nice car too.'

'Not as nice as yours was,' I said, pushing past her and wondering why, exactly, I was feeling so much more vindictive than normal. I expected it was a slight edge of nervousness, which was worrying to say the least, but there wasn't much I could do about that. I hadn't really had much choice other than to keep Colton relatively close – he knew my secret. Not the hazy details surrounding my sister's time off school and subsequent time frozen in the education system, but the fact that I'd knowingly allowed the world to believe a false carpinomen.

Worse, with a few more bits and pieces of information, he'd probably almost have worked out why.

The big secret that everyone knew but no one understood: Corin Blacksmith, serial Thomas dater, was exactly as messed up as she acted, only in a completely different way.

'Jacinta,' Colton said, leaning out the window, 'I've heard virtually nothing about you.'

'Not from me, maybe,' I said, locking the house. 'Plenty from everyone else in the Education Centre.'

'Want to ride in the front?' Colton asked her, deliberately dropping half of his smart-arse act and almost passing himself off as a normal person. It was like they were conspiring to make me as uncomfortable as possible. 'We can talk about Corin's childhood.'

I gritted my teeth and resigned myself to being wedged between Damien Elton and his eleven-year-old sister while fleeting moments of my childhood were dragged back into the present and talked over, incessantly, by two people I'd never particularly wanted to be in conversation with each other.

Jacinta was receding back into herself slightly, but she hadn't yet shut off completely – given this was the first time in years I'd seen Jacinta talk to someone she wasn't directly related to, I almost couldn't drag out any feeling of irritation towards Colton.

Almost.

'Your sister,' Colton said, sitting down next to me in the dining hall, 'is fascinating.'

'Hardly the time for your love of the dramatic, Colt,' I said, picking at my pasta and glancing over at him. 'She is a person.'

'Oh,' Colton said, reaching over and skewering a piece of my pasta, 'I hadn't realized you'd registered that.'

'Just because she acts like a robot doesn't mean she isn't capable of some feeling.'

'Halfway to school and she just *shut down*. At least you keep embittered and bitchy constantly,' Colton continued. 'She has quite the sharp tongue on her, your sister. Is that where you learned all the barb?'

'I am *not* a result of my sister's sob story,' I hissed. 'Nor am I the result of my father's death, or my dating habits. Or the government.'

'What are you a result of?' Colton asked, still grinning.

I closed my eyes briefly.

'As much as I respect you, Corin, I do not believe one *scrap* of the stuff you say.'

'I'd say I don't believe a word you say, Colt, but despite your remarkable vocabulary you seem to say nothing. In fact, I don't think you've actually told me anything.'

'I don't believe you've asked any questions,' Colton said, tilting back and eating a mouthful of his own lunch, looking entirely too self-satisfied. 'Very self-centred, Corin. It's like you *want* me to know all about you.'

'No, Colton, it's like I *don't* want to talk to you,' I said, taking up my fork again.

'If you want a topic shift, you're going to have to ask me

stuff.' Colton grinned, lolling back in his seat with half the attention of the dining hall resting on his back.

'Fine,' I said, rolling my eyes. 'Tell me about your life. Shock me. *Surprise* me.'

'OK,' Colton said, leaning forward and dropping his voice, 'here's one for you. My parents are *not* anima-vinculum.'

6

Puer Immanis

When we were in intermediate pre-level classes, we all had to tell our parents' bonding stories. It was an exercise in storytelling, public speaking and drilling the idea of soul mates further into our brains; fluffing up our heads with fairy tales so we'd remember, years later, at the beginning of the search that the years of waiting were to form part of *our* bonding stories.

I remembered feeling oddly shaky as I stood at the front of the class and retold the story my parents had garbled to me previously. Mum, who hated the sea with a passion, and Dad who lived and breathed it; meeting after almost a full year of searching despite their similar ages and living in the same country. Walden and Elspeth, the product of a generation who favoured archaic names, a one-in-a-million pairing and another love story waiting to happen. They met at twenty-three, fell in love, settled into a life by the sea and had children late.

That was, of course, before Dad died – or else they might have subtly not asked me to contribute to the class – and it was expected that we neglected to mention any marital problems or repetitive arguments, lest it smack of some rebellious streak.

Josaphine's story stood out most. Most likely because, at that time, we were nearly inseparable (this pre-dated the breakdown of our friendship by only a few weeks, now that I thought of it) and she always had such a delicate way with words – the whole classroom was on edge as she spoke, with her clear voice, about how her parents had met. Both of her parents were of Asian descent and her father, Kian, upon reading *Ling-Su* on his wrist, had decided to start his search in the Asian Section. After four years of scouring the continent for someone searching for him (and later, I discovered, in this time he also realized that he was very much gay and still resolved to find his carpinomen, only to ensure that poor Ling-Su didn't spend her whole life searching for someone who could never chalk up to the mark of a life partner), he returned to England and had more or less given up.

Then, after taking a position at one of the local archives he discovered that *Ling-Su* had gone by plain old 'Su' from the day she started at the local Education Centre and that she'd lived only fifty miles away from him for their whole childhood.

Josaphine later added that he explained to her mother that he was gay; Ling-Su had said that she was currently sleeping with a married man, and had suggested they build a life together anyway. And they'd got on so well that it had actually worked out.

And, Josaphine had finished, after his search, Kian Woolgrave had decided that *his* daughter was going to have a *European name* for as long as she lived in the European Section. And we'd all laughed.

Colton had been in that class too. His had been a lack-lustre, easy tale of two teenagers with common names being streamed into the same career and stumbling across each other.

Thinking back, it seemed so obvious that it had all been a colossal lie.

School was over and we were on our way home. 'Colton,' I said, 'you can't just say something like that about your parents, in the middle of the dining hall, and then bugger off and leave me to marinate in the thought all day.'

'Hey,' Colton said, his fingers stretching across his steering wheel, 'it's the first time you've really paid attention to me.'

There was an edge of hurt to his voice which I flat out refused to take responsibility for.

I aimed, in general, to be an unappealing prospect in terms of social interactions – to the world at large, I was a jilted, silly teenage girl who was a little too fluent in sarcasm and emotional trauma. Obviously I'd had a few of the do-gooders trying to save me – on multiple occasions – but usually after a little glimpse of how *hard* I was they backed off and left me to it. Really, I'd have fitted in more with the bitchier popular girls who had no qualms about sticking their stilettos anywhere that would help them get ahead, but the very fact that I wasn't the perfect virginal figure made me a pariah in girl world. I don't care what era you come from, or how liberal you are: if one girl defies the social norm and sleeps with someone society says they 'shouldn't', then other girls object to it. I had two occasions of sleeping with the *wrong* Thomas under my belt (and they probably thought I had a third too), which meant I was a source of contempt, shock and petty insults. Sympathy too. Apparently I should be mourning the loss of my virginity like it actually mattered. Apparently I was the victim in all of this.

That left me with the male population of the Education Centre. Friendship with members of the opposite sex wasn't discouraged as much as it was accepted that pesky hormones and feelings could get in the way of things. Some girls believed the myths that it was impossible to fall hopelessly in love with anyone but your soul mate, but the majority of people believed in a lower-level love that you could believe yourself to be in and was probably only going to end up badly (such as with Jacinta and Brett). I thought the whole lot of it was bollocks.

The main reason I didn't generally have male friends, other than my basic hatred of all people, was that they tended to get the wrong idea. Just because I had slept with two people, it did not mean I was going to sleep with all people.

Anyway, I lost respect for most of the people within the

Education Centre when they started gossiping about my sister while she could quite clearly hear them.

I did not, ever, suggest to Colton Furnish that I wanted any form of friendship with him. I accepted his lifts to school during the period when Jacinta was back in hospital and I accepted lifts for the duration of ration week, but I never *said* that I was interested in his life or his wellbeing.

I had agreed to go to his house after we were finished at the Education Centre that day only because I wanted to know about his parents. I didn't need people. I didn't want anything to do with people.

'Cut the crap,' I said. 'You've lured me to your house and kept me in suspense all afternoon. What the hell do you mean, they're not anima-vinculum?'

'I like literature,' Colton said, 'but that doesn't mean I talk in metaphors. I mean, they don't have each other's names on their wrists. I mean, they are *not* soul mates.'

'And they're married?' I asked, feeling my throat tighten slightly. My mother called it my perpetual desire to be contrary (and said that it was sure to dissipate the second I found my match), but I'd always found the stories about non-soul mates inherently fascinating. I had *no idea*, however, that I could be so close to a *puer immanis* (monstrous child) without even registering it.

Obviously I'd always dismissed the notion and the statistics the government dealt out about pueri immanes and non-anima-vinculum relationships. As the children of such relationships were legally considered 'monstrous', it wasn't any great surprise that the government passed them off as doing badly in school, being streamed into mediocre careers and contributing nearly nothing to society. The divorce rates for anima-vinculum relationships were practically zero, but showed some tiny percentage of failure (which was usually blamed on serious mental illness or one of the couple being sent to prison), whereas the much smaller number of non-anima-vinculum relationships were reported to have a seventy-five per cent rate of failure.

'Never knew you were so conservative,' Colton said, raising his eyebrows at me. 'Going to write me off as unnatural?'

'Unnaturally forthcoming,' I corrected, shifting around in the car seat so I could face him properly. 'Are you crazy? No one knew about this.'

'I'm encouraged to keep it quiet,' Colton said. 'My parents make that clear.'

'I bet they do,' I said, frowning.

'It's for my own good,' Colton said, 'to prevent me being treated like a second-class citizen.'

'Now that's literature,' I said, reaching up to run a hand through my hair, wrist guard pressing into my neck. 'Colt, it's not common knowledge because you're clever and attractive. And that's just not what people expect from someone whose parents aren't soul mates.'

'Don't make me blush, Corin.' Colton grinned, his finger tapping distractedly against the steering wheel.

It seemed almost absurd that Colton Furnish was a puer immanis. He was one of the most self-assured teenagers I'd ever met in my life – even though I was about as cynical about the whole anima-vinculum thing as you could get, I'd pinned down the immanes as being awkward and unsure of themselves.

Even if it was only because they were looked down upon by society.

Even if it was just because they believed themselves to be unnatural.

In Level Four history class I decided that the worst part about slavery, racism, sexism and all the prejudice and hatred in the world was not the fact that people were oppressed and hurt and held back, but the fact that they might believe themselves to be worth *less*. That, to me, seemed like the real tragedy – to encroach on another's freedom of thought in that way. No one should feel like they were worth anything less than anyone else.

'What happened?' I asked. 'In storytelling you said they met as teenagers and were streamed into the same profession.'

'That's true,' Colton said, shrugging slightly. 'They were best friends. They fell in love.'

'But their soul mates,' I implored. 'What about *them*?'

'My mum's called Amy,' Colton said, watching my reaction carefully, 'and my dad's called Jak. Two of the most common names in the world. By chance, both their carpinomens were quite common too: David and Emily. They decided that . . . well, whoever they were, they would find another Jak and Amy.'

'They're cynics?' I said, my voice dropping lower, so that I was only just whispering. It crossed my mind that my reaction to this could be very telling, but I wasn't sure whether I could rein myself in. This . . . this was the most fascinating conversation I'd ever had in my life.

'Not exactly,' Colton said. 'They . . . they grew up together. They decided that years of knowing each other might just compete with their soul mate, and that it wouldn't harm anyone, that they loved each other and wanted to get married.'

My head was spinning.

We were parked on Colton's driveway, in front of a house that was almost exactly identical to mine in every respect (except for a little less garden), and I was feeling entirely wrong-footed. Inside his house were his parents. His parents who weren't soul mates, but were together anyway, who'd had children and — according to Colton — were perfectly and blissfully happy.

A sudden thought crossed my mind.

One of the rumours about the immanes was that they had no carpinomen. They were not blessed by nature, so no name appeared on their wrist when they were just a few years old.

They were wrong. Soul-less.

Maybe the reason Colton had sought me out was because I'd made my own carpinomen trail by lying, sleeping around, showing a clear lack of interest in the way the world was supposed to work. Rebelling. He didn't want to end up alone. He thought, perhaps, that I was the answer to that.

'Do you have a carpinomen?' I asked, my voice catching in my throat.

'Why,' Colton said, once again looming into my personal space, 'don't you check and see?'

I stared at him.

He held out his arm.

My whole damn life they'd drummed it into me. *You don't show anyone the name on your wrist. Not your best friend, not your sister, not your mother; no one.* Tom had been different — the context had been such that it was just about acceptable, if needy, for me to twist the catch on his guard and reveal what lay beneath ... but even if I had really been jilted, I wouldn't have dared to breathe a word about the real name on his wrist. I wouldn't.

Tom's reaction to the moment had crystallized it for me — the sheer nakedness you felt was so uncomfortable, so off-putting, so unnatural.

I ... I had shown my wrist to Josaphine. The only thing I'd had to give her in response to an asexual anima-vinculum partnership was a part of my soul. I remembered the raw, uneasy feeling of clumsily undoing the catch on my wrist guard and allowing her to look at the flesh underneath. I remembered the way it had torn me up inside, knowing that she knew who I would spend the rest of my life with. It had capsized our friendship into awkwardness and a hellish limbo. We hadn't lasted another month after that, and I was absolutely and completely sure that the name on my wrist was burned onto the back of her eyelids, that she'd dream about it, be aware of it every single time she looked at me.

I felt the same about seeing Tom's carpinomen.

And here Colton was, offering up his wrist for me.

He didn't know what he was doing.

'I can't,' I managed to say, even though it irritated me to admit it. There was no reason why I should be afraid to look at his wrist. In reality, all a wrist *was* was a portion of skin that separated the hand from the arm, with a single name written across it. It was nothing to be afraid of. All of this anxiety was just conditioning.

'Relax,' Colton said, retracting his wrist and grinning. 'That's a ridiculous rumour. Of course I have a carpinomen. It's a great one too.'

I breathed a sigh of relief, leaning back and pressing my head into the back of the passenger seat.

'I bet mine's better,' I said, beginning to relax again. 'Mine's brilliant.'

'Of course it is.' Colton grinned. 'I could hardly imagine the other piece of your soul being anything other than spectacular.'

'So you believe it, then?' I asked. 'Even though your parents . . . you believe in soul mates?'

'Believe?' Colton asked, looking slightly confused for a second. 'Corin, it's not a matter of believing anything, unless you're talking about those mad cynics. They just chose otherwise.'

Mad cynics, right. The ones they occasionally showed on the news, once in a blue moon, when political disturbance was at its greatest. I had every clip of every one stored on my tabloid, filed under the name of various pieces of homework I'd long since deleted, clogging up my assigned memory space with illegal data about *conspiracies* and faults in reasoning.

Most of the clips that made it to the news did make them look mad — wildly comparing us to snails and questioning why snails didn't have a name printed across their shell.

'They gave me a common name so I could choose too,' Colton said, 'so, not too unimaginative. Just practical.'

'My parents had common names — at least, they were common for their generation. They're not so fashionable now,' I said, my throat feeling tight. 'They were still searching for ages. Hence, I got an uncommon name.'

'Not many Corins,' Colton agreed.

'I'm on top,' I said, trying to filter some of the thoughts out of my head lest Colton should pick up on them. 'My preferred position.'

'I'll bet.' Colton grinned. 'Now, do you want to meet my parents, or not?'

The two-child rule led to extreme uniformity in housing. It wasn't communism so much as practicality; the government had decided that there was no real need for people to have differing sizes of houses (there was some disparity in regards to area and status, but nothing madly different) and thus the blueprint for the whole country was three bedrooms, one bathroom, a basic kitchen-diner and two other rooms which could be used for whatever purposes the owners decided on.

The layout was exactly the same as my house, all of the Thomases' houses, and Josaphine's house, but the decoration here was so akin to my old home near the sea that I felt like I was walking into the past.

'You OK?' Colton asked, sending me a worried glance. 'Not about to get all prejudiced on me?'

'Is this a time machine?'

'Sorry?'

'Nothing,' I muttered. 'Just . . . reminds me of somewhere.'

'All right,' Colton said, grinning. 'Well, Corin Blacksmith, meet my parents.'

Colton pushed open the door to the kitchen.

Any desire to meet Colton's parents stemmed purely from the knowledge that they were not anima-vinculum, but they seemed just the same as any other couple or anyone else's parents: Amy Furnish was leaning against the kitchen counter, baby in arms, looking slightly unimpressed but nevertheless pleasant, while Jak sat at the kitchen table scanning through his TTC.

I'd never really looked at Colton properly before, but was now faced with that disturbing jerk of familiarity in seeing his features mixed up and scattered across his parents' faces. Amy was the one with the dark skin, dark eyes, dark hair but very delicate feminine features, while Jak reminded me of the caricature Vikings from pre-level history class — slightly ginger hair, pinkish skin, round ruddy cheeks and a rugged strength that I saw in Colton sometimes. Colton's features seemed to favour his father's side (although it was difficult to tell whether that was just because they were both male), though he had more of his mother's colouring.

'Hi,' I said, standing in the doorway feeling awkward.

'Corin,' Jak said, glancing up from his TTC. 'How's your sister?'

'Fine,' I answered, remembering what Colton had said about his father working on my sister's ward. I didn't recognize him, but then I usually only dealt with the nurses. The doctors only arrived to deliver important news and my mother was considered the party who needed to hear that news, not me. 'Hope she doesn't cause you too much trouble.'

'Better than most,' Jak said. 'Sweet potato chips or stew, Colton?'

'Chips,' Colton said. 'Corin's curious about your relationship.'

'Colton,' I said, interjecting with a shake of my head.

'It's OK, Corin.' Colton grinned, crossing the kitchen and plucking his sister out of his mother's arms. Addressing his parents, he added, 'She's usually all smarm and rudeness. If I'd known this would get you to be polite I might have tried it earlier.'

'Social etiquette is worth adhering to,' I said, which was a lie. He was right. I walked through life without giving a damn about most of the general rules I was supposed to care about, but that didn't mean I didn't understand the delicacy of broaching something like *this*. I had no intention of sounding bigoted or prejudiced, when I was very much the opposite, but I wasn't quite sure which words would cause offence.

'This is little Ava,' Colton said, glancing down at his baby sister with clear adoration.

'Didn't you grow out of show and tell after intermediate pre-level classes?' Amy asked, rolling her eyes. 'Forgive my son, Corin, he's showing off all his interesting little toys. What is it that you wanted to know?'

'Just . . .' I said, feeling my voice dying slightly in my throat. Then, after a few long seconds of silence, I managed, 'How you made the decision?'

You see, I'd decided myself at seventeen that I didn't want to be found as someone's anima-vinculum. Then, I'd been on my second Thomas (Tomas, as it had been), and I concluded that, beyond the comfort of physical intimacy and losing myself in the basic structure of teen relationships, I didn't want anything to do with other people.

People were complicated and messy.

People let you down.

People did stupid things for stupid reasons.

People expected you to be a certain way and rejected you when you were even slightly different to those expectations, but continually demanded that you accepted their flaws and understood *them*.

'I was always practical,' Amy said, glancing between her husband and her son with a slight smile. 'I didn't want to search when I'd already found something good enough. I'm not saying that, maybe, there's not another person out there who's better suited to me than Jak, or who might understand me better, or who might . . . *fit* me better, but . . . I don't think that could eclipse years of being best friends.'

I couldn't believe how calmly this woman was reacting to the fact that I knew enough about her life to make it significantly more difficult. If everyone knew the truth . . . well, it was rarely reported on the news, but there was hate crime against non-anima-vinculum couples, the immanes were bullied, they were threatened . . . in a world where most prejudice was now illegal, these were the select group of people who it was still acceptable to hate.

Humanity always had to hate someone. It gave them a purpose, I supposed, and made many feel like they were worth more. There are too many people for everyone to be satisfied with being equal. People always want to be more significant than the blips in history they are.

'Why are you curious?' Amy asked. 'Thinking about rebelling against your carpinomen?'

'No,' I said, glancing down at my wrist guard and thinking of the name underneath. My future. The supposed other part of my soul. The bit of my soul that I never wanted to go searching for . . . I'd still get out of town, after I'd finally been streamed somewhere, but only because I wanted to travel and *see* things. Not because I wanted to find anyone.

I was just fine by myself.

'It's a bigger decision for you,' Jak said. 'Name like Corin. There's what, couple of hundred of you?'

'One hundred,' I said, 'in the UK.'

I didn't like to think about the consequences. That somewhere my carpinomen would be searching for a girl who didn't want to be found, that they might never give up, or think that I was dead and mourn a life they'd been sure they would have.

'Don't pay attention to us,' Jak said, still not looking up from his TTC. 'We're an odd bunch. There are not many parents that have kids eighteen years apart.'

'My fault,' Amy said. 'Convinced I wouldn't be conventional. Then went and decided to cash in all that life could give me at the last minute, so to speak.'

'She hasn't got her carpinomen yet,' I said, glancing down at Ava's bare wrist, not sure whether or not I felt repulsed or drawn to her tiny fingers, huge brown eyes and exposed barely-there wrists.

'Not for a few years yet,' Amy said, glancing at her daughter with obvious love. 'She's too young.'

'I saw your look when Mum asked if you were considering rebelling,' Colton said, in the privacy of his bedroom. 'You're not actually considering it?'

Colton's room was full of a mishmash of memorabilia: evidently he was a lot more well-travelled than me if the collection of *actual* paper postcards was anything to go by (the sort that were a mark of history rather than something to actually send; I'd never known anyone rich enough to send a real paper postcard, although I'd received more than my fair share of digi-postcards, which were nothing more than messages with a photo attached when you really thought about it). There were little moulds of plastic too, mocking the old monuments that used to clutter the earth before it was deemed too unsustainable.

'Is this an Eiffel Tower?' I asked, running my finger over the plastic and turning to face him.

'Yeah,' Colton said, 'but that's not an answer to my question.'

'Why do we, as a species, knock things down and still consider them important enough to set them in plastic?'

'Sorry my choice of souvenir offends you,' Colton said, 'but it's like a symbol over there in France. It's scrawled across everything. The city planning people try and incorporate the design into their buildings whenever they can.'

Maybe, because his parents weren't soul mates, their lives hadn't shrunk enough to prevent them from actually *travelling* away from the place they were assigned to for settlement.

'Corin, the question?'

'I like being alone,' I returned, hands in my pockets as I caught sight of my reflection in the screen of Colton's tabloid.

'Says the girl with all the boyfriends.'

I didn't want to explain myself to anyone, least of all Colton. Even if it seemed he'd suddenly decided that we were friends – which was something I could deal with – I knew too much and thought too much to be remotely happy with letting anyone get further than skin deep. None of the Thomases had cared much about getting further than skin deep, providing I allowed them access to that skin; at the first sign of reluctance they set about trying to coax my feelings out of me, as if tricking me into a state of gratitude where I'd change my mind.

In reality, Thomas Brooks had been a prat. He took credit for being my first boyfriend, first kiss, first everything, and for being the absolute worst. What sort of human, knowing that his girlfriend's sister had just tried to slice off her own carpinomen after a non-anima-vinculum relationship gone wrong, didn't think it was inappropriate to sleep with that fifteen-year-old girl and then dump her shortly afterwards? I knew that he wasn't my soul mate, but he didn't know I knew that.

There was a sort of satisfaction in pushing people to be the worst they could be and being able to walk away without a bad conscience, because *they* were wrong. None of them knew me, either. I'd deluded them all into thinking they were using me in the worst way possible, then exposed them so they had to answer to their crimes.

A warning to boys everywhere not to pretend they're in a soul-mate relationship when it simply was not true. And to girls too. If my sister hadn't done that, she'd likely be a bonded doctor by now.

'Got to do something to pass the time,' I said, squaring my shoulders and glancing at his tabloid.

Colton was actually a decent person. He was an in-flammatory to a bad mood, but that — for the large part — was because I *wasn't* a good person and his self-righteousness got to me somewhat. He'd treated my sister like a real person (a first for many years, that was for sure), he'd given me lifts without needing to, and had even — inexplicably — told me the truth about his parents.

I just had too many secrets.

'I'm cynical,' I said, shrugging and turning round to face him. 'I can't help it.'

'Cynical,' Colton repeated. I wanted him to see what I meant with those words, but he hadn't made the association. I couldn't blame him for that.

Maybe, though, I should take a chance on Colton . . .

I'd never wanted to make anyone see before, and usually

when I found myself wanting to push myself closer to someone, I took a step back. Maybe there were things I could do. Maybe Colton would get it. Maybe I could actually work out some way we could be friends.

I wanted to try.

'You say you like literature,' I said, breaking the silence. 'Well, Colton, I might have a few books for you to borrow.'

7

Streaming

Of all the people I didn't like, of which there were a significant number, Mary Cuttleworth held a special place in my heart as one of the most detestable individuals ever to have existed. It was very rare for me to liken individuals to Hitler, and even I had to admit that it was a slight exaggeration, but I couldn't stop myself from making subtle references to the Nazis and the Heil Hitler salute whenever she was remotely near me. Of course, because that period of history was mostly censored from public view, she missed all these references entirely.

I was sure, however, that she was fully aware that I hated her and acted accordingly.

'Ms Blacksmith,' Mary said, lips twisting into a power-frenzied smile, 'it appears it's that time of the month again.'

Mary was the woman in charge of streaming me. Or, as the case had been, purposefully not streaming me and berating me for having a bad attitude and skewed priorities. Evil might have been a strong word, but the amount of pleasure she took in reassigning me to yet more Level Four classes was unnecessary and inappropriate.

'Oh,' I said, leaning forward, 'I hadn't *realized* that.'

'Sarcasm is not welcome in my office, Corin.'

'Shall I leave then?'

'You are achieving high four-point-eights in several of your Level Four topics,' Mary said, pushing her glasses up her nose in that superior way that made me want to scream. 'A four-point-nine in O and E . . . four-point-seven in literary sciences . . .'

'Yes,' I said, 'I know. Why don't we cut the crap and skip to the part where you assign me to another month of hell with the seventeen-year-olds?'

'Your behaviour has shown a marked improvement,' Mary continued, ignoring me completely, 'although it's reported that your attitude is still unsatisfactory.'

I found *life* unsatisfactory, but that didn't stop life from progressing continually. I detested how draconian the whole system was — it was downright ridiculous that a few throwaway sarcastic remarks could prevent me from ever starting a career. Unless they moved me up soon, I'd have to leave my education unfinished to go on my mock-search for my soul mate. Everyone knew that those who took a gap year usually ended up back in their previously assigned unskilled jobs and, as much as I didn't mind the Thursday evening and

Saturdays waitressing, it certainly wasn't in my life plan to continue doing so.

'I have received word that you are ready to progress,' Mary Cuttleworth said, shocking me out of my reverie.

'What?'

'You are to be streamed, Ms Blacksmith.'

'Into what career path?' I asked, forgetting to be rude and unpleasant in my shock.

'Agriculture.'

I stared at her for a few long seconds. 'Farming?' I questioned, feeling the words stick in my throat. 'I'm going to be a *farmer*?'

Farmers were usually streamed after completing a couple of Level Three classes, but certainly *not* after completing nearly a full set of Level Four classes (with good grades too, but that's what you got if you were *continually* in classes meant to stretch those who were younger than you), and were certainly *not* people like me. To farm, you had to live way out of the boundaries of the cities. To farm, I'd have to move at least an hour and a half away from my family and supposed friends (I supposed you could count Colton in this), and start manual labour without any further training.

'Indeed,' Mary Cuttleworth said, her pleasure at the ruling evident in the tilting corners of her mouth.

To cut a long story short, they wanted to get rid of me. Farming was a one-way ticket to a small life in an isolated part of the country, planning the best chemicals to put on plants and the most efficient way to produce meat. They wanted me out of the Education Centre and out of town.

'Based on *what* criteria?'

'This report states you have been selected as a result of excellent gardening.'

The gardens were another government initiative.

The history books seemed to imply that, once upon a time in a land far, far away, the government was less intrusive than it is now — where the system decides whether you're ready to move up in school and what job you will take and how much food your family requires. There was the suggestion of some darker edge to that knife too, of lots of pointless wars and people destroying their own lives through stupid personal decisions, leaving the bill for the rest of society to pick up while they ate or drank themselves into an early grave; but sometimes I thought it might be better to have a little bit more freedom.

However, people are just too damned stupid to use that freedom in a way that actually does good for the world. Still, maybe if we did have a bit more say in our own lives there'd be fewer people falling over themselves to slit their wrists in entirely political circumstances?

Each household was required to make use of the piece of land attached to their house — a garden — and plant and upkeep at least four different plants on a permanent basis. It was all done in the name of biodiversity and upholding some of the greenery the country had to offer, after we had ruined it so utterly by building on its every crevice, but on a personal level it meant a lot of unnecessary work digging in the back garden.

Before my dad died he'd taken on the gardening duties

with an odd sort of relish. They gave him more space for being good at it and they'd been just about to let him have his very own tree when the car crash killed him. For a while, Jacinta and I had maintained the upkeep of our stark garden — pansies, irises and basic plants that required little effort and less skill. Then after Jacinta's own breakdown, I'd been left to face the garden inspector alone. After one too many occasions arguing with him about the validity of a nettle's state as a plant, particularly when the other three I'd named had been grass, buttercups and a rather sorry-looking daisy which I'd actually plucked on the way home and placed in a way that made it look upright, I decided that I might as well actually follow the government regulation.

Unfortunately my begonias had been so successful that they'd offered us more land. Now we had a really quite sizeable plot at the back of our house available to us, including several trees. The long and the short of it was I was a victim of my own gardening success. For reasons I couldn't work out, though, I couldn't quite give up and let the garden rot itself to ruin. I chalked it up to some lingering sentimentality surrounding my father, or else a nature inclined to be slightly green-fingered.

As far as I was concerned, however, the garden wasn't reported to be anything to do with me. When the inspector asked who was responsible for the favourable results of the garden, Mum usually gave him a tight-lipped shrug and disappeared back into the house, and I wasn't about to claim credit for planting a bunch of flowers. In fact, I usually delivered a lot of sarcastic comments about the gardening fairy, the mystery gardener, or faked shock whenever he mentioned an intricacy of gardening – professing ignorance that shrubs even needed pruning, pretending not to know what a weed was and being unable to name anything more complicated than tulips.

'The garden isn't anything to do with me,' I said, doing my best to look suitably confused by the prospect. 'Jacinta gardens.' It was a shame to lose the mystery gardener card, but I wasn't prepared to be exiled into a life of bloody *farming* just because of some oversentimental moments re-potting tomato plants. 'She finds it therapeutic,' I said. 'She's your farmer.'

'The report says—'

'Do my fingers look green to you?'

'Well, Ms Blacksmith, maybe if you'd put forward any suggestions as to what you would *like* to do then we would not be pushing you into an unsatisfactory career path.'

'I've *said* what I want to do,' I said viciously.

Mary Cuttleworth smiled slightly and began flicking through her TTC, the corners of her mouth becoming sharper as she found the file she was looking for.

'Two years ago, you said you wished to be streamed as a *therapist*. When asked why, you said so you could do my job. I then pointed out I wasn't a therapist and you said, *Exactly, Ms Cuttleworth, so stop trying to talk to me about my feelings.'*

'My point remains.'

'One year ago you reported a desire to *drown yourself in a stream.'*

'That was a play on words,' I said. 'Stream as in *career* stream, and stream as in *like a river but smaller* stream.'

'Perhaps we should stream you into comedy?' Mary Cuttleworth said savagely. 'Six months ago, you requested to be streamed into prostitution.'

'Actually I think I said I'd rather sell my body than remain in Level Four classes for another month,' I said, hunching in the seat. 'There's a difference.'

'In January, three months ago, you said you'd like to be, I quote, *anywhere but here*.'

'I stand by that.'

'The problem, Corin, is that you do not act like a young woman ready to embark on a career.'

'No,' I said, folding my arms over my chest, 'the problem is *you* were streamed incorrectly. Clearly you have as much skill at your job as you do at recognizing sarcasm. I'm not sure I feel *safe* with my life left in your hands.'

'You started fights,' Mary Cuttleworth said, her voice rising several decibels. 'Several. Unladylike conduct. An inability to form friendships. A lack of interest in humanity. A lack of compassion towards your sister.'

'I did not start fights,' I said, glaring at one of the motivational wall projections. 'I simply stopped people spreading rumours about my sister. Besides, none of those qualities are really screaming *farmer* to me.'

'I will talk to the higher-ups,' Mary Cuttleworth said. 'Now, Corin, please get out of my office.'

'Gladly,' I said, giving her a sarcastic salute before leaving her office with a scowl on my face.

Of all the outcomes of my meeting with Mary Cuttleworth, none of which were sure to be pleasant, I certainly hadn't been expecting to be pushed into *farming*. I wasn't naïve enough to assume this was a chance encounter; the government didn't legally attach us to our TTCs and control every aspect of our lives for no reason. A dispute with a fellow student, Josaphine, when I was still just a kid had been enough to warrant government intervention. They watched you continually, and apparently my recent behaviour was upsetting someone.

I made a note to carry on with whatever it was.

'So they tried to stream you into farming?' Mum asked as we sat over dinner. 'Why?'

'My streamer didn't seem to know either.' I shrugged, looking at my food and trying to forget how hilarious Colton had found the whole ordeal. 'She said she'd talk to people.'

'At least they seem inclined to move you,' Mum said, sending me a suitably accusatory glare.

'What have you done to upset them this time?' Jacinta asked (a moment of surprising clarity from Jacinta, who usually refused to talk during meal times). I was slightly surprised by the sharp expression on her face. She looked a lot more *human* than she normally did.

'Jacinta,' Mum said, glancing at her.

'She's right,' I said, surprising myself. 'I've got to have done *something* for them to be punishing me with farming.'

I wondered, maybe, whether they'd got wind of the fake carpinomen trail I'd been planting for four years . . . it seemed very unlikely, but given Colton was aware of this fact my secret wasn't necessarily as well kept as it used to be.

I trusted Colton. I didn't know how it had happened, but I actually did. Internally I was still trying to explain away my growing relationship with Colton Furnish by the fact that he was a *puer immanis* and I was far too interested in all things wrapped up in that, but if that was the case it would be a lot easier to draw the line between where intrigue ended and actual like of his person began.

Colton couldn't help being a nice guy. Obviously his moral compass was stuck so far up his own arse that I was surprised he was actually able to take hanging around with someone as morally impermissible as me (the fact that he knew about my transgressions with the multiple Thomases bothered me – shouldn't he be more alarmed by how easy I'd found it to use them? How little I cared that I'd turned Tom into a social pariah? How amused I was at the hundreds of gay rumours that had sprung up out of my *him* comment?), yet he seemed to enjoy constantly seeking me out.

He continually offered me lifts that I often took, because anything that meant I didn't have to spend as much time with Jacinta was a serious bonus for me. He joined me for lunch almost every day. He read the books I'd downloaded onto his tabloid. He seemed perfectly accepting of my attitude problem and general hatred of just about everyone and . . . I respected him for that.

Almost.

'Maybe it's your friendship with that new boy,' Mum said, raising her eyebrows at me. The message was clear there. If you sleep with this one, there's no excuse. Even I couldn't pass off getting confused between *Thomas* and *Colton*.

'Colton never did anyone any damage,' I said, but it got me thinking. Maybe this sudden desire to turn me into an agricultural goddess was due to Colton being an immanis? 'He's far too bloody moral.'

'You could do with some more of that,' my mother said, her prim expression showing years of stress over our careers. Honestly, you'd have thought by this point my mother would have accepted that I was never going to be exactly the child she wanted me to be. She described my appearance as aggressive, but generally thought I was aggressive all round: bitter, complicated, too many layers for her to dissect, and far too realistic for someone of my age.

Unlike Colton, I just couldn't get a grip on optimism.

I made a note to find out who Colton had spent most of his time doggedly following around before me and asking them whether they were chased off by the prospect of some odd, unappealing career that involved moving into near isolation.

Then again, that sounded like it required far too much conversation with other people.

'What did you think of Shakespeare, then?' I asked, flopping down onto Colton's bed and glancing around his room with a grin. 'I thought it would suit your flair for the ridiculously dramatic. Plus, he reminds me of you — lots of words without really saying anything.'

I'd fallen in love with Shakespeare completely by accident. The samey endings should have turned me right off, but I found myself willing to forgive Shakespeare for being a slave to the conventions of the time simply because of how utterly creative his writing was. I'd never read anything that pushed the boundaries of language so much until I'd stumbled across a full copy of *Much Ado About Nothing*. Besides, it was amusing to try and predict exactly *how* the story was going to get to a point of mass marriage or serial suicides.

'Definitely a lot of words,' Colton said, fingers drumming across the desk in that way they did whenever he was nervous. It reminded me of exactly the way he'd looked before he'd accused me of creating a fake carpinomen trail, so it wasn't too much of a mad guess to predict what was coming next. 'So . . . Corin, I don't mean to be a stick-in-the-mud when I say this, but those books . . . aren't they illegal?'

'It depends how you look at things,' I said, bringing my knees up to my chest and watching his reaction carefully. This was crucial. I was going out on a limb here. I'd literally given Colton Furnish enough power to ruin my life . . . but, then again, I knew he was a puer immanis and there wasn't much more life-ruining than that. Still, this was my test.

I'd tested all of the Thomases in turn. They'd all failed. Thomas one had failed the moment he'd tried (successfully) to get his hands in my pants. Tomas had failed after a heart-breaking load of garbage I'd spewed about Brett not being my sister's soul mate, because he hadn't immediately backed away and admitted the truth that he knew we weren't soul mates either. Tom failed just by becoming boring much too quickly. I might have tied myself to any of them if they hadn't confirmed my suspicions about the general state of humanity. I might have done.

'Looking at things from a not-wanting-to-be-locked-up-in-prison perspective,' Colton said, 'how do the books fare?'

'I haven't been arrested,' I said.

'How the hell did you get hold of ancient literature like that?'

'Flirting, mostly,' I said, smoothing my hand over the edge of Colton's pillow distractedly.

'Why didn't I guess that?' Colton asked, shaking his head slightly. 'Explain, Corin.'

'I . . . well.' I paused slightly, heart beating at an uncomfortably high rate. 'I have a certain contact.'

I had never told anyone about this. For one, I'd never had any reason to. No one had ever expressed an interest before. And then there was the fact that it was illegal, and very telling . . .

Usually, when I told my mother I'd skipped school to stay at home and read, she assumed I meant reread one of the trashy bonding stories that had been published and vetted as acceptable for school children (read: no explicit sex). There were a few crime novels. A couple of thrillers. Poetry. Boatloads of vomit-inducing poetry that had made me consider cutting out my heart or butchering my wrists beyond recognition. Instead, I was at home searching out old, illegal texts and *devouring* them. I even liked stories where the sexism was palpable – which, honestly, was the case in pretty much all literature *ever* – because they were real in a way that reality never seemed to be.

'Tell me more.'

'Actually,' I said, 'I have a few. I . . . I don't buy the news.

They don't tell you the full story. I was . . . frustrated, so I started browsing the searching files. There was this guy there who worked for the Media Network, said he was searching for this girl called Raychel. So . . . since I was sixteen I have pretended to *be* Raychel.'

Colton shook his head. 'You pretended to be Raychel?'

'Yeah,' I said, pulling out my TTC and finding one of the many files of messages from Ean Broth, a morally question-able executive of the Media Network with significant access to the things I wanted. Colton crossed his room, leaning over and watching as I scrolled past the hundreds of messages. 'They're not all kid-friendly. Oh, especially not that bit . . . but the footage of the D'livere suicide was highly monitored.'

'You have that footage?'

'It's not pretty,' I said. 'Don't watch it before bedtime.'

'What about the actual Raychel?'

'Oh,' I said, and grinned. 'Well, I figured that out pretty quickly. As it turned out, he'd already met a Raychel search-ing for an Ean, but . . . in his words, "I refuse to believe such a prudish uptight woman could be my soul mate; clearly she was fabricating a carpinomen in order to sleep with me." She left him to "become a lesbian" — all very hard on him, poor Ean.'

'Doesn't he want to meet you?'

'Ah,' I said, 'well, I took a few numbers off my age.'

'How many numbers?' Colton asked, taking the TTC out of my hand and pausing at a particularly embarrassing stream of messages (I'd run out of books, Jacinta had been driving me crazy and my mother had banned me from leaving the house except for attendance at the Education Centre — I'd *needed* something to read).

'I said I was nine.'

'Nine? Corin, this stuff is practically pornography . . . and he thinks you're nine?'

'No,' I said, pulling the TTC out of his hand and pocketing it. 'Now I'm twelve.'

'That is horrific.'

'I never claimed he was a nice contact,' I said, shrugging my shoulders slightly, 'and at least it buys me a bit more time. He shouldn't want to meet me until I'm at least fifteen, for fear of a public scandal. That's another three years of . . . getting the news. And stuff like books.'

'And you think that's worth it?'

'Shakespeare,' I said, standing up. 'The Brontë sisters, Harry Potter, *Lord of the Rings*, Plato, the Bible . . . you can't claim to love literature and not think it's worth it.'

'Why?'

That was the killer question. That was the part of this that was most difficult to answer.

I could take the easy route out and try and put into words how much I loved stories, but that was only part of it. Yes, reading books was one of the few things I actually honest-to-God *enjoyed*, but part of that enjoyment was derived from the fact that it was illegal.

'Because I can,' I said. 'Everything about this whole world is dictated to us. I know it's not much of a rebellion, Colt, but . . . the knowledge that I have access to more information than I'm supposed to helps me sleep at night.'

8

A New Position

'So, what can this guy get me then?' Colton asked, making his usual point of reaching over and stealing some of my lunch. Technically that wasn't allowed. Everyone was given exactly the amount of food they needed to maintain a healthy and efficient lifestyle, but I doubted anyone would take any complaint I made against him seriously.

A shame really, because ever since I'd brought up my contact Colton had been obsessively asking me about him and there was only so much I could take before I started to go crazy. Not least because he kept asking me questions in relatively public places, turning me into a paranoid wreck.

Still, it *was* nice to have some company during lunch.

'He can't get *you* anything,' I said, 'but he is willing to encourage *Raychel* in her budding career as an investigative journalist.'

'And he doesn't suspect you're a fake?'

'I'm a very convincing twelve-year-old,' I said.

'If by that you mean the spelling mistakes in those *sex* messages then—'

'They're not sex messages,' I interrupted, 'and would you mind keeping your voice down, Colt? I'd rather *not* be arrested.'

'He should be arrested for inappropriate liaison with underage girls.'

'I'm not underage,' I said.

'He *thinks* you are.'

'He also *thinks* he's my soul mate. The law is surprisingly lax about things like that.'

'And you'd know because?'

'Because I'm interested,' I said, 'and when I'm interested, instead of sitting around mourning the lack of surviving literature like some people, I go *searching* for things.'

'For trouble,' Colton said. 'You're determined to get yourself in a mess, aren't you? Is that what all the Thomases were for? To get you into trouble?'

'No,' I said, 'they weren't.'

'But,' Colton said, 'let's just say you'd met your carpino-men and you wanted to start a relationship with him . . . no one's going to believe you're anima-vinculum because you've spent four years creating a rather convincing story that it's Thomas.'

'You didn't believe it,' I said, shrugging my shoulders.

'Yeah.'

'Well,' I said, 'why wouldn't everyone else notice?'

'I just don't understand *why* you did it.'

'Oh God,' I said, rolling my eyes, 'it's not that complicated, Colt. My sister had a boyfriend and I wanted one. Thomas was the most common name in the book. I was young enough to pass off as a naïve little girl and, lo and behold, no one was too fussed about taking advantage of that.'

'You can't really accuse them of taking advantage,' Colton said.

'Can't I?' I asked. 'Why the hell not?'

'Because you were lying to them too.'

'That's not the point,' I said, setting down my fork. 'Look, Colt, if you want to get all judgemental and moral on me, that's fine, but I don't regret any of it.'

'Why sleep with him?' Colton asked. 'Them.'

'Why *not*?' I asked heatedly. 'Because I wanted to, because I wanted to break the stereotype, because I could, because it felt good. Pick your reason.'

'No need to get defensive,' Colton said. 'I'm just asking you a friendly question.'

'Laden with judgements,' I said. 'What's the big deal? Considering sexism is supposed to be long dead it's a bit bloody rich to have all these questions directed at me. Why did *they* do it? Why did *they* sleep with me? They knew I wasn't their soul mate. Worse, they thought I believed we were soul mates, which makes their actions all the more damnable. I slept with Thomas Brooks because Jacinta was in the *mental hospital* and I was trying to prove a point. I didn't expect him to immediately dump me after the event, which was a bit late for guilt, if you ask me. Tomas Prandle was an exercise in proving to myself that I wasn't some hideous creature after I realized that all my friends were detestable pieces of work who liked the drama much more than they liked me. Tom Asquith was just me seeing what I could push a supposedly nice guy to do and, anyway, I didn't sleep with him.'

'You just exposed his carpinomen and started a rumour that he was gay?'

'His rep would never have recovered if he had slept with me,' I said, 'and besides, he won't do it again.'

'I doubt he'll be thanking you.'

'You forget I know his carpinomen,' I said, 'and she'd definitely thank me.'

'So you don't feel guilty about it?'

'No,' I said viciously, 'I really don't. Nor do I feel guilty about pretending to be a twelve-year-old to exploit an old, lonely man with access to bits of the news I want to hear about. Why should I? If people are prepared to be so heart-less and horrible then how is that my fault?'

'You push them to it.'

'I'm not that strong,' I said. 'It's a little nudge, if anything. They'd *like* to blame me. I'm not poisonous, Colt; people are toxic all by themselves.'

'Are you going to try and push me?' Colton asked.

I thought about the bits of literature and the bits of in-formation I'd given him. I wasn't *pushing* Colt. I just wanted him to engage his brain and *think* about the information I was setting in front of him. I wanted him to read Shakespeare and Harry Potter and all these novels and words and see the common denominator in all of them.

I hoped, with the same things that had opened my eyes up to the truth, Colton might actually be able to see me. If anyone was going to, it would be Colton.

I couldn't deny that I was still testing him, but it was definitely very different. I had some basic faith that Colton Furnish wasn't the usual worthless, immoral type.

'It'd take something to get past your stabilizers,' I said, glancing away from him. 'Now, for God's sake, can we move away from dissecting my actions and on to something a little more interesting. I thought I saw Jacinta smile today, but I think it was just a weird angle in the mirror.'

'I thought I saw you smile yesterday,' Colton said, 'but it turned out you were just being sarcastic.'

'Hilarious,' I commented dryly. 'Now piss off and let me eat my lunch in peace.'

'So,' I said, 'how come you've been in non-specific streaming for such a long time?'

I'd become used to spending time in Colton's bedroom. Usually we spent the time discussing whatever novel I'd had Colton read the night before. There was something really wonderful about being able to have conversations with someone about these things, because all those ancient words made me oddly hopeful that perhaps there was a chance that things could be a little better. I wasn't under any delusion that real life could ever be like fiction, because fiction was full of heroes and flawed characters who saw the error of their ways, of crimes being solved and love conquering evil, whereas life was full of crappy broken people who were just trying to make do with what life threw at them.

'The literary stream is full,' Colton said. 'It's not so bad, really. I think I've probably nearly completed as many Level Four courses as you—'

'No one has completed as many Level Four courses as me,' I interjected, sighing as I lay back on Colton's bed and glanced up at the ceiling. There was nothing all that special about the ceiling — just an expanse of white plaster — but ever since I was little I'd found the practice of staring at ceilings satisfying. With nothing but white to concentrate on, the rest of my explosion of thoughts had enough room to breathe.

'Well, no,' Colton agreed, 'but . . . they've offered to stream me into a number of careers. Never farming, though.'

'They only try to fob off the really special people into agriculture,' I said, running my hand over Colton's bedcovers. 'It takes serious skill.'

'I'd really like to stay in education.'

'Why?' I asked.

'You obviously like learning,' Colton said, 'or else you wouldn't have put yourself at risk by getting into all this . . . stuff.'

'You don't know the half of this "*stuff*",' I said, thinking of all the news footage and sob stories, all the conspiracy theories and outlawed literature and otherwise illegal material that was filed away on my tabloid. If anyone ever searched it,

I'd be arrested straight off. Sometimes I was surprised I hadn't been already.

'I imagine not,' Colton said. 'Budge over, Corin.' I obediently shuffled to the end of Colton's bed, pressed against his wall. 'I'd really like to be streamed into a Masters,' he said softly.

'Wow,' I said, feeling Colton's body heat as he lay down next to me. I breathed in a whiff of his aftershave, turning my head so that it rested on his shoulder. 'I didn't realize anyone liked the Education Centre that much.'

'I'd be over at the University Complex,' Colton said, 'but apparently the need for literary academics is minimal.'

'Well, that's hardly surprising,' I said, 'given how little the government appears to like lit. How come they haven't forced you into another career?'

'Aptitude for the subject,' Colton said, 'and they don't know what to do with me.'

I wondered briefly whether the reason they were keeping Colton in limbo was because he was an immanis, but I decided not to voice my concern. I was entirely sure that the thought had occurred to him hundreds or thousands of times before. If they could hold me back because I was difficult and my sister was crazy, they could hold him back for being a child they never wanted to have existed.

The government had a lot to answer for.

'They asked me about the gardening today,' Jacinta said, grabbing my arm as I passed her in the corridor at home and pushing me against the wall. It was true that if she'd not actively stopped me from passing her I wouldn't have bothered to stop and listen. 'I denied any involvement.'

'Good,' I said savagely. 'It's nice to have the government ignorant about one part of our lives, even if it's just who waters the pansies.'

'The whole world isn't against you, Corin,' Jacinta said.

'You are.'

'There's nothing to be ashamed of,' Jacinta said, her eyes narrowed slightly. 'You can admit you like gardening. You can admit that you miss Dad.'

'It was you that told me not to mention him in the house,' I said, feeling my face twist into an expression of displeasure. 'What do you want?'

'You've been spending a lot of time with Colton Furnish,' Jacinta said, releasing my arm and receding back into herself slightly. Her eyes remained alert, though, fixed on me and watching every single shift in expression.

'And?'

'*Mum* thinks it's good you've finally made a friend.'

'Well,' I said, 'are you thinking about attempting it? Is that what this is about? Because I don't have enough words in my vocabulary to scrabble together advice that might help your cause.'

'No,' Jacinta said, her voice cold. 'I think you're getting yourself onto dangerous ground.'

'And you'd know all about that, wouldn't you?' I retorted.

'I think Colton likes you,' Jacinta said, eyes narrowing slightly, 'and I think he likes you too much.'

'So?'

I'd suspected something of the sort myself. Usually it took a lot for someone to be prepared to put up with my less appealing qualities. While I had originally chalked it up to my being mysterious, what with all the misleading Thomases, I had to admit that Colton had been paying attention before that had come to light. He had to have done to be able to notice it all.

Boys deluded themselves into liking me all the time. It wasn't for any real reason other than the fact that I wasn't some blushing virgin waiting to be swept off her feet by her soul mate; mostly no one really bothered making an attempt on me (thinking themselves exempt from the select group of people with the right name to be considered), but they certainly looked.

I wasn't pretty. I didn't dress provocatively. They looked because I was just slightly more accessible than the rest of the damn population. As if, just because I'd slept with someone else, I might be willing to sleep with them too. Bloody nonsense, of course, and I thought too much of Colton to place him up there . . . but he'd definitely shown a few sparks of being a little *too* interested.

'I can handle it,' I said, moving away from Jacinta and glaring at her. 'I certainly don't need *you* stepping in.'

'Really?' Jacinta asked, taking an uncharacteristically bold step into my personal space and staring me down. 'Because I think, Corin, that you like him a little too much too.'

'Bollocks,' I said, but the words had taken effect; I felt a sudden need to get out of the corridor and into the safety of my own room, to hibernate away from Jacinta but also from Colton, not to have to face him for a few days just in case she was correct. I balled my hands into fists. 'You're talking *crap*.'

'You're the one getting defensive,' Jacinta all but whispered, raising her eyebrows before smiling sweetly and turning away. I watched her walk down the corridor and disappear into her own room.

Jacinta was a piece of work.

I was never sure whether she felt genuine concern, or just wanted to screw things up in my life. With my sister, it could be either. I wasn't above trying to ruin her life and I wasn't too far gone not to care about her welfare. We were equally distrusting of each other, never knowing which things were the dregs of sentiment seeping through our hard personas and which were the petty mind tricks.

I swore at her back.

While I had to admit that I hadn't willingly spent time with another person for a long time the way I did with Colton, there was almost zero chance of me actually liking him: people were a bunch of chemical reactions and cells, just a big dose of mechanisms that somehow learned how to think and feel. Most of them were selfish and crap.

Unfortunately, the truth was that while I lost my faith in humanity almost every day, it was people like Colton who occasionally resurrected my sense of hope.

Had I not been pushing him towards working out the *real* secret? Not the business about the fake carpinomen, or my father, or Jacinta, but the things that I refused to even *think* about in front of others, lest the thoughts diffused out of my head and were recognized for what they were?

I retreated into my room, viciously plugged my TTC into my tabloid and flicked the screen over to messages.

What I needed was something to distract myself, and I'd watched the pieces of video footage and read the books and gone over all the evidence a million times, consoling myself with the fact that *I'd worked it out* and they couldn't fool me again.

Hey, Ean, I typed, my hands skimming over the keys in a rush. *Anything exciting happening in the big wide world today?*

Twenty minutes and a bit of mild flirting later, I had an unaired news article about an attempted suicide in the next city block along. The reporter had tried to pass it off as a romantic story gone wrong, but I could see what it really was.

One day, I would ask Ean to dig out the story about a girl called Jacinta Blacksmith and I'd watch some nameless pretty face tell the story of how my sister's life fell apart — taking me with her — and I might just punch a hole straight through my tabloid.

'Is Jacinta in school today?' Colton asked as I sat down next to him in O&E class. I smiled at him briefly. It was actually really nice to have someone to sit next to, as much as I wouldn't admit it out loud . . . which is why it sucked that Colton had done his time in O&E and would be leaving me here to rot alone.

'No idea,' I said. 'Don't care. Not my problem.'

'If you say so,' Colton said, leaning back on his chair and

tipping it over onto two legs. 'New stock in the class today.'

'Excellent,' I returned, glancing over to Mr Robin. 'I can't wait to be told that I have the least common name in the class for the *billionth* time.'

'You could always run off and be a farmer,' Colton said, nudging me with his elbow.

'You're only making jokes because it's your last lesson,' I muttered bitterly. 'If you knew you'd be stuck in this class on repeat you'd quit with the joking around, Colt.'

'So,' Mr Robin said, 'I'm running your names through the database . . .'

'Let me guess,' I added out loud. 'I'm at the bottom.'

'Right you are, Corin,' Mr Robin said, smiling. 'Your name remains unbeaten for the most uncommon. However, we now have a new top position . . . Thomas Grit.'

'Keep your pants on, Corin,' Colton muttered, much too close to my ear.

'Always wanted to get underneath you, Corin,' Thomas Grit said, all too loudly, with a self-satisfied grin and a mock salute. *Good God*. Another Thomas. Thomas four?

'Please,' I said, twisting round in my seat to take a better look at him, 'I don't want to get arrested. How old *are* you?'

'Old enough.' Thomas Grit grinned. 'Eighteen years old and at your service, Ms Blacksmith.'

Mr Robin was slightly flustered. He was usually one of my favourite teachers, but evidently didn't know what to do when the light innuendo turned more explicit – I was sure Thomas Grit was more than happy to lower the tone of the whole Education Centre, having obviously only just finished going through the joys of puberty, but I'd be damned if I had to stay in a class with him for much longer.

'So . . .' Mr Robin said, clearly trying to draw the class's attention away from the spectacle that was my love life, 'our resident top and bottom . . . supposing we have a Thomas/Corin carpinomen pairing . . .'

The class cheered. I rolled my eyes and crossed my arms over my chest, sending a bemused look in Colton's direction. He looked as though he found the whole thing a lot less amusing than me.

'. . . we have an estimated search time of seven months.'

'Did it take you twenty-one months to find all three then, Corin?'

'Congratulations,' I said dryly, 'you've successfully managed pre-level mathematics. Would you like a trophy?'

'Round that up to twenty-eight months,' Thomas Grit said, ''cause Corin's just bagged herself number four.'

'Give it a rest, Grit,' I said, turning back round to the front of the class and sending a worried glance in Colton's direction.

The usual easy-going line of his lips had distorted into something that seemed to indicate displeasure. I elbowed him and raised my eyebrows, silently asking him, *What?* Colton shook his head, shrugged and turned away from me.

I had to admit that I'd always thought the bonding books were trashy as, but that didn't mean I didn't have the residue of poor writing, weak and vapid characters and the overused sub-standard plot still ingrained onto the tissue of my brain.

And if I hadn't wanted to deny it so much, I'd have come to
the rather uncomfortable conclusion that Colton was *jealous*.

Which was, of course, disastrous.

And not only because it meant Jacinta had been right.

9

Father's Day

Maybe the best solution to the problem hadn't been to ignore the quasi-friendship Colton and I had formed, avoiding the dining hall, consuming my lunch in my car and pretending not to receive any of his messages, but then again I wasn't exactly known for my rational decisions. I just needed a little bit of space. More to the point, Colton clearly needed some space if my sister and earlier suspicions were right and he *actually* liked me. I hadn't been able to face him the next day and then, suddenly, that had become not being able to face him the day after or the day after that. Then two weeks had flown by, I'd returned to my previous status of social recluse (and I'd almost *missed* it) and found myself beginning to relax again.

Unfortunately it seemed likely that, at some point within

the fortnight I'd been outright ignoring Colton Furnish, he'd actually noticed.

I hadn't necessarily *decided* to stop ignoring him; it was just that — of all the days in the year — there was one that made me feel so goddamn lonely that I physically couldn't handle it. And, given that I was a heartless bitch who pushed people away, I didn't have much choice of people to run to. The plan to exploit his good nature for the day and then resume my silence sounded cold even in my head, but there was a level of hurt after which a human was prepared to do anything to make it stop — pull out their own hair, stop eating, take a knife to their wrist, pull the blade across their skin until it bled. Or simply become a horrible person.

Once a year, the feelings all caught up with me and nearly swallowed me whole. When you're drowning, you'll accept help in whatever form it comes. You'll sell your soul to stop the water filling up your lungs.

In one of my illegal books, I'd read about a tradition of celebrating mothers and fathers on a particular Sunday of the year (back when Sundays meant something religious and special — nowadays religion was all but dead and, from what I could work out, the bits that had survived the years weren't anything like the things the Bible and the Qur'an and the like had been aiming for) and the idea had always struck me as having some merit.

I couldn't abide birthdays. Given a year was, basically, the way us humans decided to carve up time (with a little help from lunar movements, it had to be said) the idea of celebrating birthdays always seemed to smack of the usual human arrogance that made me chafe. I was all for celebrating continued existence, but surely you could celebrate every day as a new personal best in living through consecutive days . . .

Motherhood, though, was something that I deemed worth celebrating. And since losing my father, the concept of fatherhood had rattled around my brain and stained it slightly. I had no idea what day Father's Day should have been on, but I picked the day my father died. April the eighth. There was no way I could escape the emotions that came with the day anyway, so I made a point of forcibly acknowledging them each and every year.

This was ten years. A whole bloody decade.

I hated feeling emotionally vulnerable and alone. Colton was a willing warrior to fight that feeling; a knight in shining armour and all. He'd practically been begging for the job.

'Haven't seen you for a while,' Colton commented in that would-be-casual tone of his when I approached him in the car park after school.

'Well,' I said, somewhat stiffly, 'you're not in O & E any more.'

'You are.'

'Well done, you've successfully stated the obvious,' I added dryly, twisting my hand through his for a second to retrieve his car keys — his expression at that was priceless. I guess he hadn't anticipated key theft as my first move. 'I'm driving.'

'Taken any prescription drugs lately?'

'Not for at least twenty minutes,' I said, unlocking the car and climbing into the driver's seat. 'Hey, your car looks even better from this angle.'

'Is that it?' Colton asked, slipping into the passenger seat and holding his thumb out, just beyond the scope of the recognition pad. 'No word from you for a fortnight and now you want to drive my car?'

'You want an apology or something?'

'I'm not that optimistic,' Colton returned, 'but an explanation would be nice.'

'I can talk and drive,' I said, 'but I'm going to need you to start the car, Colt.'

'And squander the only power I have over you?'

'Oh, Colt,' I said with a grin, 'you've got plenty of power over me; now, lend me your damn thumb before I have to remove it by force.'

'I used to come here with Tom,' I said quietly, as we pulled up in the car park facing the beach.

Colton looked slightly white thanks to my erratic driving, but I hardly regretted it. Sometimes I just had to put my foot down on the accelerator and hope to leave everything else behind; to drive so fast that everything else just fell away.

I wanted to get away. I wanted to be able to move somewhere. I wanted to fall out of the system and be given an actual choice of which way to ruin my life, rather than having it dictated for me. Surely that was what all this was about — I wanted my own opportunity to screw up and have to reap the consequences.

'Which Tom?'

'Don't be an arse,' I retorted. 'This is where I took off his wrist guard.' I traced the edge of Colton's wrist guard with my fingers distractedly, running my middle finger over the catch: for a second it was like he was half daring me to take it off, to expose his wrists to the outside word and take in what was written there. It wasn't like he hadn't done it before. He'd offered up his wrist and said, essentially, *Take a look, Corin.*

I pulled my hands away and stretched them across the surface of the steering wheel. 'Want to go sit on the beach?' I suggested, suddenly bursting into motion and half tumbling out the car.

It suddenly seemed too intense and serious in there, and I couldn't deal with that. Not today.

There were days when I'd swear blind I didn't have a single feeling left in my body, but today it was as though I could easily drown in the grief of it all. It wasn't because of my father. He was just the tip of the iceberg. I was mourning Jacinta's sanity, my mother's happiness and my inability to see the good in things. I contemplated what would have happened if an unlikely car crash hadn't taken away my father's life and whether Jacinta would still have fallen for a boy called Brett, whether I'd have slept with Thomas and Tomas and if my mother might not have had to watch us both self-destruct.

'What's with the emotional bipolar, Corin?' Colton asked, following me down the steps to the beach. I skipped ahead, half tripping down the last three, and then hurried to the edge of the water. 'Corin?' Colton called again, catching me up just as I was pulling off my shoes. 'What's going on?' he demanded.

I stepped into the water. I'd done this back when I was tiny. We'd lived further away from the Education Centre and nearer to Josaphine; in the months during which we were inseparable, we'd chase waves and tell each other myths we'd heard about mermaids and pirates. When I was seven, I didn't think I'd ever want to move away from the glorious place where the sea met the land; I thought I would be content, for ever, to stand on the edge of England knowing who I would marry and that someone else would dictate my career. I didn't want anything more than that.

Now, I wanted fucking everything.

'Can you just . . . go with it for a couple of minutes?'

Colton made a face but started to pull off his shoes. Mine were already clogged up with sea water, but I couldn't find it within myself to care. Colton pulled off his socks and dropped them in his shoes, taking a single tentative step towards the edge of the sea.

Then I grabbed his wrist and pulled him towards the horizon.

'It's this date,' I explained, later, when we were both sitting on the sand side by side and much too close. Colton was distractedly running a finger over the back side of my wrist, just before the bit where the wrist guard concealed my flesh. 'It's . . . my dad. Ten years ago.'

'When he died?' Colton asked.

'Yeah,' I answered, drawing a circle in the sand so that I didn't have to look at him. 'I do not like this date.'

'So,' Colton said, 'what actually happened?'

'Freak accident,' I said, looking up and watching the sky. It was hard to believe that we'd damn near ruined the world when you came face to face with a sunset; there was something inherently beautiful about watching the sky bleed pink and orange, the sun receding into the sky, the darkness creeping over the world. 'He was driving to work. The car malfunctioned . . . the wheel slipped off; the car went spinning out of control, the engine sparked up, boom. Toasted father.'

There were things I wasn't going to mention. I wasn't going to talk about the ghosts of my father I saw, sometimes. It had only happened a handful of times and I wasn't nearly crazy enough to believe I was actually seeing him. I knew my dad was gone. I knew the occasional sightings were because I missed him.

It was always near the beach. I could probably chalk that up to the fact that the beach was my go-to place when life started grating on me. After Jacinta was admitted to hospital, I'd haunted the coastline myself and thought I saw my father half a dozen times before I realized I had to pull myself together. There's no real use in wasting time in places that used to hold good memories, because it only reminds you the good times are dead and gone; after that fortnight, I decided I was punishing myself by going to the beach and my mind was joining in by adding the hallucinations.

Jacinta had punished herself enough for the both of us, so I hadn't come back for nearly a year.

Still, it would always be the place I came to remember my father.

'So you were nine. Rubbish age for it to happen,' Colton commented, his fingers still brushing over the back of my hand. 'Old enough to understand death.'

'It's not that hard to understand,' I said. 'It happens.'

'What did your mother do?'

'Nothing,' I said. 'Within two days we moved across to the other catchment area. I used to live within walking distance of this beach. Mum pretended it hadn't happened until I was nearly twelve, then suddenly the old photos went up on the wall and she stopped acting like Dad never existed.'

'Did you and Jacinta talk about it, at least?'

'Jacinta and me, talk?' I questioned, stretching out my legs. My legs had been wet up to my knees and now the sand was sticking to my skin, but I liked it. Mum had always described the experience as unwanted exfoliation, but the beach was one of the few things Jacinta and I had in common. Our father, too.

'You can't always have had such a . . .'

'Non-relationship?' I finished for him, glancing back at the sky. The sun had all but disappeared, leaving a rich, bloody red in its wake. Soon, there'd be no light at all. 'Jacinta thought it would be better for Mum if we didn't mention him.'

'So you just didn't talk about it, ever?'

'I'm talking about it now, aren't I?' I said.

I glanced at Colton. He looked good in the light of the sunset – it highlighted the caramel tones to his skin, the suggestion of copper tones in his otherwise dark hair, made his dark eyes look all the more dramatic.

He probably looked so good because I was all but starved of affection. Sure, people could call it dysfunctional all you liked, but the Thomases served their purpose – it was one of those facts of nature that physical contact with another human being made you feel more solid, more grounded in the present, and reminded you that you weren't so repulsive that no one wanted you near them. My mum had given up cuddles when we'd learned how to walk, I wouldn't dream of hugging Jacinta, I eschewed friendships and my dad was long dead. The only chance I had of being held or touched or having someone casually draw circles on the back of my hand was through whichever Thomas wanted me at the time – or now, Colton.

'Ten years too late,' he murmured.

'We were made to talk to therapists,' I said. 'They didn't know what to make of me.'

'No one knows what to make of you,' Colton said, grinning. 'You're a walking enigma.'

'I'm simple,' I retorted. 'I want *everything*, but feel let down by just about *everything*.'

'Am I letting you down, then?' Colton asked, his eyes turning towards me and fixing on me intently. I wasn't used to the scrutiny. I didn't like my face to give away too much. I barely liked people knowing things about me at all . . .

Of course, Colton was slightly different because I had *tried* to share certain things . . . but he hadn't got it. He'd missed half the hints I'd been trying to drop. He didn't think like me.

And he liked me. I didn't want him to like me.

'No,' I lied easily, leaning back on my arms and turning my gaze, once more, towards the sky, 'but I'm waiting for you to.'

'Maybe that's why you have such difficulty with people,' Colton said, his voice light but his expression a little too serious. 'You set them up for failure.'

Well, I thought, the world set me up for failure. I wasn't the one who started this. None of this was my fault.

Colton drew a heart in the sand. 'Give a guy a chance,' he said, before scattering it with the palm of his hand. 'No one's perfect.'

That was one philosophy I could definitely believe in.

'Look,' I said, as I pulled up on the street before my house so that I could talk a bit more, 'sorry about all this.'

'Corin,' Colton said with a smile, 'honestly, you don't have to apologize for acting human for once.'

'Don't I?' I asked with a wry smile. 'I meant about ignoring you for a little while back there and then enlisting your help to get through the worst day of the year.'

'I quite enjoyed it, in the end,' Colton said, looking far too pleased with himself.

'Right,' I said, running a hand through my hair and making a mental note to cut it soon. It was creeping past my jawline, making my face look softer. 'Well, I just wanted you to know . . . I don't make a habit of dragging people to the beach and talking about my feelings.'

'I know,' Colton said. 'I've known you for a while.'

'And I'd rather we never mentioned my father ever again,'

I said. Normally, I didn't feel the need the explain myself to whoever I spent the day with, but Colton *knew* things about me. In fact, Colton Furnish knew a *lot* of things about me that, frankly, should terrify me into never leaving the house again.

'OK,' Colton said, 'relax, Corin. I understand.'

'I'd rather you didn't,' I said truthfully.

Colton half laughed and shook his head, fingers running across the edge of the window. 'I know that too.'

'Well, that's sorted then,' I said. 'Time to go home.'

'Expect so,' Colton agreed, with a sad, knowing sort of smile.

'Start me up then, Colt.'

Colton leaned over to press his thumb against the recognition pad at the exact moment I turned to face him; we were caught in a sudden, awkward moment with our faces much too close. Colton had his left arm outstretched, his right hand holding onto the edge of my seat and I was staring up at him feeling oddly shell-shocked.

Neither of us moved and the moment continued. Then the moment had continued for so long that there was only one way out of being stuck there for ever.

Colton's left hand closed around the steering wheel and then, of course, our lips touched. Then they collided. And suddenly I was kissing Colton bloody Furnish.

It was strange, how everything always seems to end like this.

It took about a minute for me to realize that this was quite possibly the worst thing that had happened since Jacinta had thought it would be quite nice to get off with Brett Jones, and then Colton's hand dropped from the top of my seat to my waist and it took another thirty seconds for me to remember it again. Another few seconds to work up the motivation to do something about the terrible thing that was happening, and then about four seconds to throw open the door of the car and declare, 'I'll walk home from here,' and shut the door behind me.

'Corin, damn it!'

The edge of my coat was caught in the door. I tried to pull it out before frantically trying to reopen the door to release myself. Too slowly, apparently, because by that time Colton had leaped out of the car and run round the front.

'Can't we talk about this?' he suggested, stopping just in front of me. The bastard pressed the button that locked the door and raised his eyebrows. Forgotten I'd given him the keys. Bleeding typical.

'That definitely classifies as harassment,' I muttered, tugging at my coat again. 'Trapped against my bloody will, Colt.'

'*You* can leave,' Colton said. 'I'm just keeping your coat.'

'It's not your colour,' I said, yanking on the material angrily.

'Angry isn't your colour, either. Just hear me out.'

I tore my gaze away from my coat and glanced up at him, only to find that he was much closer than I'd previously anticipated. Course, now I'd kissed him, he'd be dead set on invading my personal space.

'What?' I demanded, only to have Colton smile and then

reach forward and kiss me again. It didn't feel so awful now I was out of the car and it was easy to let myself get pressed up against the bodywork. 'This isn't talking,' I pointed out, frowning at him.

'What can I say? You're irresistible.' Colton grinned, his fingers threading through mine.

'Most manage it,' I returned coldly.

'You say that,' Colt said, 'yet you've got a whole generation of men called Thomas quaking in their boots.'

'And a Colton.'

'Evidently.'

'I'm sorry, Colt, I just think this is a recipe for disaster.'

'We both know the terms,' Colton countered, finger tracing the edge of my wrist guard in that frustrating way of his. 'I think I probably know you better than anyone, Corin.'

'Not saying much,' I said, still frowning. 'There's still plenty you don't know.'

'It's not like I'm suggesting we get married.'

'Just that we date,' I said, 'and *pretend* that we're anima-vinculum, even though the whole damn world thinks my carpinomen is Thomas. Which is the bit that is supposed to sound appealing?'

'The bit about me.' Colton grinned.

I smiled despite myself, reached forward and kissed him of my own accord this time. 'Persuasion isn't your forte, is it?' I asked but, damn it, it was working slightly — after all, it's not like I ever followed the rules. And it wasn't like I had much to lose, either. I could stay in control of this easily.

Surely it was only different because Colton was more

aware of my terms? The other Thomases were all convinced that *they* were the ones wronging *me* in some way, when actually I was fully using them for my own devices. The problem with people knowing that you're using them was a side order of unfortunate guilt.

I took a step backwards.

'Look, Colt . . . Tom Asquith? He said he loved me and look what I did – as far as the girls are concerned, making him gay, I turned him into non-boyfriend material. I am not a nice person.'

'He loved you?'

'God, I don't know, I'm not a mind-reader. I know what he said.'

'I think I can probably handle you, Corin.'

'Really?' I asked irritably. 'You've brought it on yourself then.'

'What?'

'The bit when this ends terribly,' I finished.

'As long as it doesn't end immediately,' Colton said, grinning.

Then I kissed him again, letting him wrap his arms around me, noses touching and foreheads pressing together.

I can't deny it: I hated being dependent on people, but loved the feeling of being needed. With someone kissing me, I could stop thinking about everything else. It was another occasion where I felt like I had control – the government could expect me to marry the name branded on my wrist, they could try and force me to become a bloody farmer, they could take away my freedom and force me to fit in a box that

I was never designed to fit in — but I could still kiss whoever the damn hell I liked.

Of course, this was a natural disaster waiting to happen. But, as always, it was nice not to be lonely for a little while.

10

A Deviation into the Emotional

'Thanks for coming to pick me up,' I said, locking the house behind me as I walked down to Colton's car.

'I'll pick you up any time.' Colton grinned.

'For that comment,' I said, 'I'm driving. Out, Colt.'

'I don't trust you with my car,' Colton said, allowing me access to the driver's door anyway. 'Poor thing.'

'She'll live.'

'I'm not sure I will,' Colton said, before seeming to realize that the comment was a little off base given the events of yesterday. I rolled my eyes and shook my head at him — people needed to quit with these damn sensitivities. A comment about car crashes was not about to turn me into an emotional train wreck; I was tough. 'Where's Jacinta?' Colton asked, to punctuate the silence.

Jacinta, on the other hand, was not tough.

'Elsewhere,' I said curtly, running my hand over the steering wheel and glancing at the screen. 'I want you to start the damn car, Colt.'

'OK,' Colton said, stretching out his hand to the recognition pad, but not quite touching it, 'but only if you tell me where Jacinta is.'

'I'll cut your thumb off if I have to, Colton.'

'You'd get blood on my pretty upholstery,' Colton said. 'You wouldn't ruin something so beautiful.'

'If you're so interested in Jacinta, why don't you go date *her*?'

'How can I? I don't know where she is.'

'Hilarious,' I said. 'Fine, but get on with it or we'll be late.'

'With your driving,' Colton said, pressing his thumb against the pad with a grin, 'I don't think lateness is much of a possibility. So, where is Jacinta? You haven't just abandoned her in bed?'

'She can drive,' I said, turning onto the main road and testing out the accelerator. I could feel Colton tensing beside me, so I let up slightly; besides, not every day called for maniac fast driving. It was inefficient in terms of petrol. 'But, no, she's in the hospital again.'

'Ah.'

'Right,' I said. 'Attention whore.'

'You know, your sister is actually pretty sick. Maybe you should . . . ?'

'Try to be understanding?' I suggested. 'I *have* tried. I

failed. Anyway, I got back to utter bedlam last night. She was
. . . bad. Mum was upset, obviously.'

'Bad how?'

'Shaking,' I said. 'Scratching at her wrist guard, going *on
and on* about Brett. It wasn't even because of it being April
the eighth, either; apparently some boy in the FE centre tried
to grab her arse and she just went *ape shit*. She only got home
half an hour before I did, having dumped the car four miles
away and stumbled home . . . well, at the first sign of self-
injury we're supposed to send her back to the ward, but Mum
figured it might just be the anniversary – amazingly, she did
seem to note the date herself – and thought Jacinta would be
OK later. But she wasn't. Just got worse and worse.' I turned
left, glancing up and down the road and feeling my shoulders
tense uncomfortably. 'So, Mum's freaking out. Jacinta was
going nuts. I was about to drive Jacinta to the hospital . . .
Mum was halfway through getting me added back onto the
insurance when Jacinta then started going on about me
spending too much time with you . . .'

'Sorry,' Colton said, holding up his hands slightly.

'Hardly your fault,' I muttered. 'Anyway, Mum called the
hospital and they sent someone out. Then Jacinta was convinced she didn't need to go. They had to sedate her.'

'Wow,' Colton said. 'Are you OK?'

'Perfectly,' I said icily. 'You fail to see that none of this
is my problem, except for my prolonged separation from
my car.'

'If you say so,' Colton said. 'You can swim in denial for as
long as you like.'

'Thank you,' I said. '*De Nile* is the longest river, so I should imagine I'll be happy swimming there for a very long time.'

'Terrible pun,' Colton said. 'Archaic. Tired. You just let me know if you need to stop treading water, won't you?'

'Consider it done,' I said, inhaling. 'I generally find it better to dissociate myself from the whole Jacinta business. It's easier to be angry than to be upset.'

'I don't think that's very healthy.'

'Look,' I said, taking a corner a little too quickly and braking, 'you do what you've got to do to get by. I cannot continually be affected by every single one of Jacinta's episodes, because it would saturate me emotionally. It is *unremitting*, and it's probably not going to get any better. Any day, she could wake up and be sick. I could track her moods and worry myself into madness every moment of every day, if I should want to. My mother manages it. I could try and work out what all of it *means* and question *why* and *blame myself* but it would kill me to care that much.'

'But you do,' Colton said. 'You *do* care that much.'

'I give up on you,' I said as we reached the car park of the Education Centre. 'Leave me to drown in peace.'

'Fine,' Colton said, 'but we're going home via the hospital.'

'No, we're not.'

'Stop being self-centred,' Colton said. 'I have to go pick up Ava.'

'Right,' I said, distracted. 'Fine.'

'Although I *am* fully intending to visit your sister too, and it's going to be a bit awkward if I go on my own.'

'Yeah,' I said, pushing the car door open, 'then I'm

going to be finding someone else to give me a lift home.'

'Really?' Colton asked, locking the car and running the keys through his fingers. 'Because I wasn't actually aware that you had any friends.'

'Thomas Grit,' I said. 'He's going to be my next conquest. Bit of an idiot and practically still in nappies, but he has got a *very* nice car.'

Colton grinned.

I had intended to talk about the prospect of our relationship during the car journey here, but evidently that hadn't happened and that put me in a rather difficult position. I did not think Colton was up to the task of facing the entirety of the Education Centre's collective shock, nor did I think it was a particularly wonderful idea to start acting remotely couply around other people when we had about fourteen hours of being a *thing* under our belts.

'I can't deal with people's reactions today,' I said sharply, 'so just . . . just don't do anything.'

'If I can take you out tonight?'

'Can't,' I said. 'I've got to make sure Mum's all right. Tomorrow?'

'That's bearable,' Colton said, squeezing my hand – just for a second – before the pressure was released and he walked towards the Further Education block without me. He had an Additional literary studies class for the next two hours, while I didn't have any classes until Level Four astronomy (death in lesson form) right before lunch.

I sent my sister a vaguely abusive message about how her selfish actions had meant I had to get up earlier than necessary, to which I got: *Leave me alone, Corin, I can't deal with your crap right now.*

I'm coming to visit you later, I returned.

Bring me something sharp that I can stab you with.

I smiled and pocketed my TTC. See, Jacinta was fine. As long as she still sent me abuse, there was definitely no need to worry about anything.

Jacinta looked worse than I'd seen her for a long time. Then again, last night had not been a common event for years, and even then the occasions when Jacinta *really* lost it were minimal. Her greatest talent was shamming being OK and living life despite the dark thoughts that clouded up her mind. I was the same. My second therapist (the one assigned to help me deal with seeing my sister's wrists bleeding out in the sitting room) had said that Jacinta and I fell back on a state of pretending to be OK after witnessing our mother do exactly that after our father's death.

I had always suspected that she might have a point, but I never thought understanding the particular intricacies of the ways I was messed up was particularly helpful; largely thanks to several bouts of therapy, I could now recognize whenever I was about to screw up and fall into the familiar pits of my own self-destruction, but I certainly didn't know how to stop them. Instead, it led to me justifying it and almost expecting to fall into the same patterns of behaviour. How could I *help* but lie and test people if it was all I knew? Then I didn't have to take responsibility over it. Then I didn't have to deal with it.

'Hi,' I said, shoving my hands into my pockets as I took a step forward, kicking the leg of the seat next to her bed to make it a decent angle. I sat down heavily and tried to look at her without really seeing her. Taking in her red eyes, pale skin and maddened expression only made the whole thing more real, and Colton a little more right.

'Corin,' Jacinta said, her expression stony.

'You OK?' I asked stiffly.

'Hmm,' Jacinta said, glancing up towards the ceiling. Her hands made a tiny convulsive movement, as if she'd meant to run the bitten stumps of her nails against her flesh, before catching the impulse and stopping herself. Damn.

'So who's the guy I'm murdering?'

'Please don't,' Jacinta said, her voice lacking its usual strength. 'You are neither calculating nor careful enough to successfully murder someone.'

'Surely I only need to be calculating and careful enough not to be caught,' I said. 'What happened?'

'It wasn't his fault,' Jacinta said, balling up her fists in the material of the sheets before releasing them again. 'I shouldn't have *reacted*.'

'No,' I agreed, 'but you did. It's OK. Tell me what happened.'

'He . . . was just being misogynistic,' Jacinta muttered, clearly agitated. 'Just being a prick, really, but he . . . he just made some stupid remark and grabbed me and I just . . . I couldn't have anyone touching me.'

It was funny how Jacinta's response to a broken heart was

to not let anyone physically touch her and mine was distinctly the opposite.

'So, you punched him, right?'

'We're not all *violent*, Corin,' Jacinta said.

'Save me the lecture about not being ladylike,' I returned, pulling my chair slightly closer and resting my hands on the corner of her bed. 'So you, what? Walked out of school? Drove around the block driving yourself crazy with thinking so much? Dumped the car?'

'I ran out of fuel,' Jacinta said. 'I wasn't planning to walk.'

'I filled it up a couple of days ago,' I said. 'Where the hell did you drive to?'

'The beach,' Jacinta said, fingers still restless and longing to reach out and pinch, pull, bruise her own flesh.

It had never occurred to me that the beach might be a special place for Jacinta too, even though it was obvious that it would connect to the same memories for her as it did for me. The three of us building sand castles, jumping waves and battling with melting ice creams . . . Jacinta always ordered vanilla and I always ordered chocolate. I'd mock her for picking something so *boring*, but the chocolate was always too rich for me to eat all of it. We'd always, without fail, swap ice creams halfway through. It had never occurred to me before that Jacinta might have secretly ordered the vanilla for her little sister's benefit.

Suddenly, I almost wanted to mention the fleeting, dreamlike glimpses of Dad. Colton had really made me think about the hundreds of things Jacinta and I probably should have talked about back when we were acting as each other's support systems. This seemed like one of those rare opportunities to bring those things up, but even now, with Jacinta in a hospital wing, I was loath to make myself vulnerable in front of her.

I settled on saying, 'We must have nearly overlapped.' It gave her enough information to fill in a few of the gaps, yet didn't flesh out my emotions enough for her to really understand. It was a sad but somewhat unsurprising fact that I still couldn't trust her with my emotions.

'And then . . . the crash site.'

'Jacinta,' I said, my voice low and uncommonly soft. I didn't do soft. I wasn't good at it. I'd never visited the place where my dad died. Because of where our new house was located, there was almost no reason at all that you'd end up there, unless you went to seek it out. I didn't fancy seeing the tarmac and trying to trace out the accident in my head: I'd see the ghost of his blood, the burned-out wreckage of a car, a blackened corpse that was supposed to be my father.

Mum had obviously never gone. I knew that Jacinta had taken Brett once and I assumed she'd visited it before then, but it had never occurred to me that she might have visited it since.

'They took the memorial plaque down,' Jacinta continued.

'It's probably been recycled.'

'No,' Jacinta said. 'Someone had torn it off the pavement. You could see. There was just this *gap* and . . .'

'Well, that would have upset anyone,' I said gently, 'but that's still only half a tank of fuel.'

'I just needed . . . I needed to get away,' Jacinta said; she was blinking. 'I couldn't *breathe*.'

'OK,' I said, reaching out and closing my fingers over Jacinta's despite myself. 'OK. It's . . . OK.'

'Aren't you supposed to be cold and unmoving?' Jacinta asked, staring at our hands.

'Yeah, well.' I shrugged, biting my lip. 'I'm not too good at dealing with anything on the eighth of April either. But you should know that I think your whole theatrics were bleeding *ridiculous*. You should have just *messaged* me. You definitely shouldn't have walked home.'

'And how would you have been able to help,' Jacinta said, 'with your lack of transport?'

'I'd have found a way. Somehow.'

'You don't think *anything* through, Corin,' Jacinta said.

'Says Miss Damage herself.'

'You just rush into things without thinking of the consequences.'

'I'd just rather you weren't walking miles to get home,' I said, 'particularly when it's my goddamn car.'

'You only think in the short term,' Jacinta countered, looking at me. 'You don't think about what's going to happen in ten years' time. Or ten more after that. You'd hijack someone's car, to hell with the consequences, and then be *surprised* when you ended up in St John's Prison.'

'Thank you for the character assessment.'

'I *try* to do what's best for you,' Jacinta said. 'I *try*, Corin.'

'It's not yours to *do*,' I said, twisting my hands away from hers but keeping eye contact, 'and with all due respect,

Jacinta, I don't know if you're one to make sweeping judgements about people's lives.'

'Well,' Jacinta said, 'I don't . . . I don't *care* about that.'

'No one else is going to care about it for you,' I said starkly. 'It doesn't work like that.'

'Corin,' Jacinta said, reaching out for my hand, 'I know you *hate me.*'

'I don't,' I interjected.

Jacinta used to play the mother position in the days after Dad died, back when Mum was pretending nothing had happened. As the big sister, she felt all the grit of the responsibility to keep me sheltered and safe and make sure I was OK — to hell if she was only two years older than me, she was determined that she'd take the lead. I was old enough to recognize that Jacinta needed to be useful, and to fall into the follower position and let her be the leader in our grief; she set aside half an hour each day, after Mum had put us to bed, where she'd crawl into my bed and tell me — quite seriously — that if I needed to cry this was the only time I'd have till the next day.

I was never very good at crying. For whatever reason, my emotional responses usually diverted away from my tear ducts and went straight to slow-burning anger. The only exception, I supposed, was *physical* hurt where the tears came without my permission, generally making me look like a bit of an idiot. Back then, though, I was still in such a deep-rooted shock (not helped by the sudden house move, and the *don't mention Dad* rule) that I certainly wasn't in any position to actually *cry*. However, I felt so obliged to fill that set half-hour with tears that I became an expert at crying on cue – a pinch of the leg here, a bit of concentration there – which turned out to be one of the greatest skills my sister ever taught me (very helpful with the Thomas-related situations).

I wasn't sure why I was reminded of that so forcefully now, but the memory that Jacinta and I did used to have some form of relationship was painful rather than helpful.

'Corin,' Jacinta said, drawing me back into the present, 'why shouldn't you hate me?'

'Because you're my sister,' I drawled.

'*Exactly*,' Jacinta said. 'Exactly, Corin, and I knew that you'd find me.'

That day. It wasn't the first time I'd thought over those events and come to the conclusion that my sister was a selfish bitch. There was no *question* over who would make the bloody discovery, because Mum always arrived home hours after we did. On multiple occasions I'd told myself that Jacinta wasn't thinking clearly in the moment, but it was hard to convince myself she hadn't *realized* I'd find her. And Jacinta was supposed to protect me.

'Good job too,' I said, trying to shift backwards slightly. This was very high up on the list of things that I didn't want to talk about. I'd dragged that moment of icy-cold shock and unadulterated fear into the present too many times un-willingly. Therapist two had demanded a step-by-step account of which door I'd opened and when, leading to a full account of every second that had passed between the moment Thomas reversed off the drive and I entered the living room.

'That wasn't my plan, though,' Jacinta said. 'I was supposed to crash the car, Corin. I didn't . . . I didn't want that for you.'

'You *said* you weren't trying to do yourself in.'

'I couldn't,' Jacinta said, 'and then I knew you'd find me, so I just . . . I just needed it *off me*.'

'I know, you said.'

'But I never *apologized*,' Jacinta said, pinching the sheet between her fingers. Her face was lined with agitation. Evidently I was not the only person who hated dragging this to light. Although apparently I was the only one who believed there was no need to do it. 'You are my *little* sister.'

'Only because you were born first,' I said.

Before the day Jacinta tried to slice off her carpinomen, I'd have agreed that she was your archetypal protective big sister. I lost faith in that image in the few seconds after the event.

'You always seemed a lot younger than me,' Jacinta said, 'and now you're just . . . I want to stop you from *messing things up*, Corin, but you're so stubborn and I'm just making things . . . I'm *always* making things worse, Corin, I don't—'

'Have the nurses given you something for the anxiety?' I demanded, interrupting her. 'Because if not, I want you to transfer doctors.'

'Corin,' Jacinta said, grabbing hold of my arm and digging her nails into my flesh, 'I . . . I'm sorry, Corin.'

'For God's sake,' I said, 'it's *fine*. I'm going to find the nurse, Jacinta, and she's going to give you something for your anxiety. And then you are going to stop talking about all that crap and you're going to tell me what's wrong with you *right now*.'

'Don't *leave*,' Jacinta said, grappling with the space and the need to move her fingers with nothing to grip hold of. I sighed and slipped my hand into hers, squeezing it slightly.

'OK,' I said, swallowing the twist of emotion threatening to resurface, 'fine. Colton will be here in a minute, making sure I actually came to see you. He can find his dad and get you something for this rampant anxiety, OK? And if you apologize one more time I am going to explode.'

Jacinta nodded. God, she looked small and pathetic and *not right*. I didn't like to see her with her barriers down. It made me want to resurrect them for her, wrap her up in cotton wool so that no one could get to her. I wanted to protect my sister from the whole world, but no one could protect her from herself.

It was illogical, because I was happy for myself to self-destruct . . . but Jacinta's self-destruction *hurt* a lot more than I was willing to admit to anyone. Colton could rehash the conversation as much as he liked, but there was no explaining how it felt to watch your sister want to die.

'Budge over, then,' I said. 'This chair's bloody uncomfortable.'

Jacinta dutifully shifted over on the hospital bed, not letting go of my hand as I transferred my backside to the bed.

'You're staying the night?'

'Even if I have to OD.'

'This is exactly what I mean,' Jacinta said, her voice regaining a little of its strength. 'You never think *long term*.'

'It depresses me,' I admitted, looking up as I heard the

footsteps that marked Colton's return. 'Hey, Colt, can you grab a doctor? Jacinta needs some meds.'

'Sure.'

'I . . . I regret a lot of things, Corin,' Jacinta continued.

'Good,' I said. 'That's probably for the best if you want to avoid being sectioned.'

'But, most, I'm sorry for the effect that my decisions had on your life. You didn't . . . you shouldn't have ditched all your friends just because—'

'You weren't there,' I said, trying to stop my shoulders from tensing in case Jacinta became aware of how little I wished to talk about this. 'You didn't hear what they said.'

'And you're the only one allowed to mouth off about me?' Jacinta suggested.

'Exactly,' I said, glancing up as Jak Furnish entered the ward, Colton just behind him. Colton looked a little too domestic with the lump of Ava in his arms, but I had better things to be worrying about than any of that right now. It seemed my sister's latest outburst was significantly worse than I was willing to think about.

A brief explanation to Jak, along with the fact that Jacinta was quite obviously *very* stressed out was enough to secure some drugs (although by the look on Colton's face he was less than convinced . . . but then, he'd seen me right after Jacinta's last bout in the hospital having *taken* some of her drugs, so I'd let him off).

'Would you like to stay with your sister, Corin?'

'Yeah,' I said. The pills were placed in Jacinta's hand, and she examined them suspiciously for a moment before swallowing them. There was a time when Jacinta was on so many prescriptions that she'd probably rattle if you shook her (and I wanted to shake her, repeatedly), but these days they only gave her pills to take when she was in hospital. Although maybe not after this stint? 'If that's OK?'

'Fine by me,' Jak Furnish said.

'I won't be needing the lift, Colt,' I said, not quite meeting his eye. He was reeking with the assertion of being right about me, as if it were actually some great big secret that I *did* care deeply about my sister. Of course I did. That didn't stop me from resenting her with a passion, but of course I *cared*.

'You need a lift tomorrow morning?'

'Um.' I glanced at my sister. 'Sure, thanks.'

Then he was gone. His dad disappeared shortly afterwards, leaving the two of us alone.

'Next year,' Jacinta said, her hand still hot in mine (and a little more restful now), 'we spend the eighth of April together. No men.'

'Agreed,' I said, although I had my doubts. I doubted that Jacinta would be around next year. Presumably she'd have to start searching at some point . . . she wasn't ready for it now, clearly, but she'd have to be ready lest she stay *alone* for ever – but I didn't think the higher-ups would let that happen without serious interference. I might have given in to the pressure and agreed to become a farmer by then. I might be on my fake-search. I might be doing anything.

Even if we were still living together in our tiny house, our relationship would probably be in shreds. I wasn't optimistic enough to assume that we were capable of standing by each other for long. Highly emotionally-charged situations were somewhat different, because Jacinta was made up of so many of the same chains of DNA as me, and had shared so much of my childhood, and was so much a *part* of me, that it was near impossible to walk away. Just because I loved Jacinta Blacksmith, my crazy sister, didn't mean I wanted to put up with her every single day.

'Ten years,' Jacinta said. 'It . . . it doesn't feel like that long ago.'

I disagreed. To me, the photographs in the hallways were from a completely different era. I wasn't the girl who forced herself to cry for a set half an hour a day to appease her sister, nor was I – really – the girl who'd stayed on the beach until way after sunset, flat-out refusing to go home until I'd built one last sand castle. That wasn't *me*, because that girl still had hope and still believed in this future that I just couldn't buy into now.

'I remember the ice cream,' I said, as the drugs began to seep into Jacinta's system and ease out the tension in her arms. 'You always ordered vanilla.'

'You could never finish a chocolate,' Jacinta said, smiling slightly (and how long had it been since I'd seen my sister actually smile?). 'Dad used to order toffee, or butterscotch or something fancy like that.'

'And Mum never came,' I filled in. 'You can't claim ownership over ruining my life, Jacinta. Those mistakes are all mine.'

'You like owning them too much,' Jacinta said, eyes flickering shut for a split moment, 'as though ruining your life is a worthwhile cause.'

'If someone gave me a better one . . . ?'

'Colton seems nice,' Jacinta said. 'Should I like him?'

'Yes,' I said. 'I'd prefer it if you did.'

I wasn't about to make the same mistake that Jacinta had made. I knew the terms as well as Colton did and, besides, I had my own weapon of being distrustful and having more knowledge than Jacinta had. Sometimes it made my blood boil that, if only Jacinta had acted differently, none of this would have happened . . . and sometimes it made my blood boil that she'd never thought it through properly.

Then again, Jacinta and I had always been like that. We were continually in battle with each other for attention and a sense of superiority; to feel like we were the one who was in the lead. Running alongside the need for competition was a protective desire to block out all harmful influences from the outside world. We wanted to know as much about the other as possible, while not allowing them to know a thing about ourselves (in case it worried them). We were the archetypal siblings — half hating each other, half loving each other, always bickering and always pushing. Always *worrying* and wanting to be distant and then wanting to be close again.

I didn't like people knowing too much about me, and Jacinta knew just about everything. Far too much shared ground. Far too many squabbles that left unintentional scars and went unresolved. Too much history.

Maybe that was why I couldn't talk to her about Dad. For a long time, I'd trusted her implicitly because she'd taken on the protective role and tried to manage our grief. She'd spent so long trying to protect me and then, suddenly, I'm standing in front of her while she's bleeding out and I'm panicking like I've never panicked before. She betrayed my trust in a way that was difficult to forgive. Every time I looked at my sister, I could see her bleeding.

'He made me come visit,' I said quietly.

'I'm glad he did,' Jacinta admitted, before her eyes shut again. I didn't think she was asleep, because her grip on my hand remained steadfast; it was OK, though. Just for a little while, I thought I might be able to keep her anchored into the present.

Jacinta was glad Colton had made me come visit.

Oddly, I was too.

11

A Brief Calm

I don't like hand-holding.

Occasionally, it was OK. I could see the appeal in it because there *was* something to be said for the solid weight of someone else's hand . . . The first Thomas used to hold my hand a lot. Being my first boyfriend and with me being a lot more naïve, I'd been more than happy to attach myself to him and follow him around. Now, the whole idea of it made me itch, but back then I'd been more than happy to relinquish some of the responsibility of my life to someone else. Then, right after Jacinta was first admitted into hospital, it felt like his hand was the only thing holding me in place . . . and I pushed myself closer, and closer, and then he let go. I wasn't thick-headed enough not to admit that hadn't hurt me, even if it was ancient history now.

Still, a lot of the time, holding hands was sweaty, needy and impractical. And I really thought Colton Furnish would be the hand-holding type.

I was taking great pleasure in being proven wrong.

Instead, Colton had a couple of his own signature moves that I suspected had been developed entirely to suit me. As much as I didn't buy into the public view of a lifetime of monogamy, I was surprised by how much I appreciated how new Colton was to this whole *dating* business. I liked that this was trial and error.

I fell into the routine of relationships a little too easily now, every so often shocking myself with the realization that this *was* different because I actually really liked Colton. It wasn't like I *didn't* like the Thomases before, because although I was pretty messed up, I wasn't messed up enough to date someone I couldn't stand to prove a point . . . it was just that I *had* been trying to prove a point.

It had been different with the first Thomas. Back then, everything was new, fresh and a little raw. By the time I got to Tom Asquith, it was more of an academic interest; an exercise in how far I could push him, testing how far I'd push myself. I'd half liked him and half thought, *Why the hell not?*

With Colton, I was constantly trying not to think about the hundred or so reasons *why not*. Yet, somehow, I'd still fallen into another relationship, which was so different it was hard to measure them on the same scale. So whenever I found myself falling into the rhythm of one of those past relationships, it was nice that Colton did something so *different* that I found myself remembering that I actually cared about him.

Colton liked to trace shapes on the back of my wrist, just above my wrist guard. I always thought that one odd, because it served as a reminder that we *weren't* carpinomen. I found reassurance in that reminder, but I could never understand why Colton would. He liked to lean over and kiss the corner of my mouth when I was driving his car. He had this special smile for whenever I insulted him, and frowned whenever I insisted on keeping the relationship a secret.

However, my favourite was his hand-holding replacement. We'd checked into a restaurant near the beach — far enough away that we'd probably avoid being spotted, but close enough that we tucked ourselves into a corner just in case — and Colton was distractedly pressing the pads of our fingertips together.

He traced out the curvature of the whorls on each of my fingertips in turn, completely unaware that he was doing it. It was probably the uniqueness that made me catch my breath slightly. Or maybe the fact that this was a completely natural gesture untarnished by the usual expectations. Normally, people were trying to reach out and *hold*, while Colton seemed perfectly content just to *touch*. The subtlety of the difference shouldn't have registered, but I couldn't stop thinking about it.

'I don't believe they're unique,' I said.

'You'll have to catch me up on your thought process there, Corin. I can't actually read your mind.'

'Shut it, Colt. Fingerprints,' I said, glancing down at our

hands and feeling an unwilling smile tug at the corner of my lips. It was just so easy to relax in Colton's company.

'It's like you go out of your way to be cynical about everything.' Colton grinned.

'Not everything. Just people and politics.'

'And fingertips.'

'And fingertips,' I agreed, lining up our fingers and pressing them together. 'Come on, there's what . . . a population of six billion? And we're just one tiny moment of history.'

'We were over nine billion for a while,' Colton said. 'Level Three World History.'

I remembered that class. It always struck me as insane that three billion fewer people existed at this moment than had previously. I knew that life wasn't a torch to be passed on, but the *absence* of so much life where it had once been seemed crazy. Of course, there'd been mass government intervention on a global scale to do something before the unsustainable ten billion mark was reached. In World History, they cited it as the first instance of global unity; the beginning of a domino effect in global policy to sort out overpopulation, the destruction of all the world resources and the eventual decision to control our careers and lives.

'Before the two-child rule,' I agreed. 'So, out of the hundreds of billions of people that existed at some point, you're asking me to believe that *no one* has ever had the exact same fingerprints as me? That every fingerprint was randomly unique?'

'So the scientists are lying?'

'Just over-romanticizing,' I countered.

'For a serial dater, you're *really* not a fan of romance. Should I be offended?'

'Always,' I said, flashing him a smile. 'I just don't buy what they're selling.'

'What do you buy?'

'In the literal sense, not much. I saved up all my waitressing money to buy my car,' I said with a grimace. The day I'd been taken off the car insurance, I'd lost any desire to acquire more stuff. There were many things you could say about my mother, but you couldn't deny she didn't know how to punish me effectively.

My car was my freedom.

'You know full well that's not what I mean,' Colton returned, withdrawing from me slightly as the waitress brought over our food. My hands seemed too cold without the pressure of his touch, but I cast that thought aside with a grimace. This was dangerous territory. 'What do you actually believe in?'

'I believe in the sanctity of privacy,' I quipped in response, taking up my fork.

'I believe that's conversation-dodging.'

'You're pushy, Colt.'

We'd both ordered steaks. The government's system of assigning food in accordance with nutritional needs was soulless and took nearly all the joy out of eating, so I nearly *always* enjoyed eating out, regardless of the company. Having a genuine choice over what you were about to consume was refreshing ... and, of course, checking into a restaurant meant I didn't have to sit round a table with my mother and

Jacinta. Avoiding members of my family was always an added bonus.

Although Jacinta and I had come to a tentative understanding, we'd still resumed our usual behaviour of irritating each other as much as possible as soon as she was released from hospital; neither of us could remember any other way to act around the other.

'And you're very hard to push. You know, Corin, you think you have this whole inaccessibility thing going on, but you're so easy to work out.'

'I doubt that,' I said, watching him carefully. 'You should eat your food. At least then you can't talk.'

'You love it.' Colton grinned, his eyes catching mine for a few seconds.

'You're prettier when you shut up.'

'So now I'm pretty?'

'Fishing for compliments,' I said, shaking my head, 'it's not helping your cause.'

'Yeah, well, with you it's like fishing in the polar ice caps. You're several feet of solid ice, Corin.'

'Ice which has mostly melted.'

Colton laughed for a few seconds and I found myself caught up in it just for a moment. I couldn't really remember the last time I'd been really amused in a way that wasn't laced with irony. I liked satire and sarcasm in an aggressive way. I didn't laugh on dates.

'I think you just made a huge human tragedy romantic, Corin.'

'Yeah, estimates say it's only, like, really partially melted,' I said, smiling, 'so please don't get too excited. There's plenty of ice left.'

'Good job, too,' Colton said, 'or else we'd be underwater.'

'This is a really accurate metaphor for my feelings on this subject,' I said through a huff of laughter. 'And this whole conversation is ridiculous.'

'Do you need to lie down?' Colton asked, with a mock serious expression. 'Because I think you just *willingly* talked about your feelings.'

'Shut up.'

'So, how's Jacinta?'

The problem was, Colton was actually concerned about her. No one but me and my mother cared about my sister, and I denied it about ninety per cent of the time. She wasn't easy to care about. She was too messed up and too broken. Believe me, I could relate.

Yet, Colton cared. Worse, he knew that I cared. I had absolutely no idea where he'd picked up the skill, but he had a way of taking all my outward barb and filtering through it to pick out some of the good bits.

He'd managed to get me in the hospital visiting my sister.

I had a few mouthfuls of steak to give myself enough time to think of a decent response.

'Not as awful as expected,' I said eventually. 'Still on the anxiety meds—'

'Without your help, presumably?'

'Yes, without my help.' It was pretty irritating that Colton had made his entry right at *that* moment, because that whole day was an event I'd really like to forget about. Even the footage of the D'livere suicide caused me an uncomfortable twinge of embarrassment (not that it stopped me following up the trail of the story, which had gone dead towards the end of February, two months ago). For the most part, I made a contrived effort not to regret things, but that had been a really poor life decision. 'I though we'd agreed not to talk about that?'

'*You* agreed not to talk about that,' Colton countered. 'I don't remember being invited to join the conversation.'

'Quit whining, Colt.' I smiled. 'Besides, I've told you what I believe in several times. *Shakespeare.*'

'I maintain your reasoning isn't healthy.'

'Fiction is better than real life. Why else would we read it?'

'Most people don't.'

'And most people are miserable.'

I didn't add that I was miserable too, because I wasn't really sure whether I had the conviction for a statement like that right then.

I was sure that in a few hours' time, when Colton had dropped me back at home, I'd find myself watching videos of politically motivated suicides on repeat. I'd be kept up half the night angry at just about everything, wondering whether or not Jacinta was awake too. I'd probably wind up sending Ean something inappropriate until he sent me some more proof that humanity was crap.

Yet, at precisely this second, I couldn't truly confess myself to be *miserable*. I wasn't happy, either, but this was progress beyond anything I could have expected a few months ago.

Which was either a good thing, or a complete disaster.

'I'm not miserable,' Colton said.

'And you read books,' I pointed out. 'What's with the fingertips thing, anyway?'

Colton aligned the pads of our fingertips again, watching our hands interact. I liked the contrast between our skin tones.

'Well, *I* think they're unique.'

'You would. Now, let go so I can eat.'

'You do have very nice fingerprints,' Colton said, withdrawing his hand again and cutting up his steak. 'Very nice tented arch.'

'That's not even a little bit right,' I countered. 'Accidental whorl.'

'Of course.'

'You're an idiot,' I said, resisting the urge to smile. 'As if you remember that rubbish. That's what, pre-level identity classes?'

Identity class was one of the most ridiculous things I'd ever been subjected to. There's nothing quite like a fortnightly scheduled hour of being taught self-awareness by a middle-aged balding man who always smelled of alcohol, especially when you're only six years old.

'You remember too,' Colton said, grinning. 'We were in the same class.'

'I'll take your word for it,' I said.

All I remembered about those classes was talking to Josaphine while Mr Wright lectured us about our blood group. I think I probably remembered more about her identity than mine.

'Well, *that's* a new development.'

'Shut up and eat your steak,' I said, taking one last moment to smile at him before I returned my attention to my food.

I didn't like hand-holding, but there was definitely something to be said for discussing fingerprints like it actually mattered. And I liked the easy conversation over dinner just as much as I liked the brief moments of skin on skin. I'd never really appreciated that before.

He wasn't expecting anything else from me, which meant, for the first time, I was being *myself* with someone else.

A modern-day miracle.

12

An Exothermic Reaction

'You know, Corin,' Colton said, arm trailing over the back of my shoulders, 'it's been three weeks. If I was less self-assured then I might start to think that you were ashamed of me.'

'It's a good job for both of us that you're an arrogant sod,' I said, reaching over and kissing him briefly. 'I just don't see this being the best move for anyone's sanity.'

'I'm reading that as "I'm ashamed of you", Corin.'

'Well, don't read, and just *listen* to what I'm actually saying.'

'It's not that easy,' Colton said.

'It really is,' I said, relaxing into his arm as his finger brushed over my shoulder. 'What you do, Colton, is you listen to the words that come out of my mouth. And then you use your knowledge of the English language and you *understand* those words.'

In my view, if there were two people in a relationship then there was a ninety per cent chance that both participants were insecure. Popular portrayals of romance usually had the two somewhat hopeless characters falling into a majestic relationship which vastly improved both their characters and led to eternal and unfaltering bliss. Well, that was a lie. Any form of relationship needed reassurance and demonstrative proof from both parties at some point (which I always considered sensible rather than paranoid) without the added pressure of wondering whether the other person still thought you were attractive.

Friendships required work. That wasn't bad in itself, because almost anything of any real value required work; it was just a shame that it took quite a bit of digging to work out which friendships were worth the effort and which most decidedly weren't.

No matter what my sister thought, the reason for my abandoning all my previous friendships *wasn't* purely because friendships took work and I was writing off anyone who dared say a thing about Jacinta, but a number of factors that all happened to collide at the same time – I'd barely felt comfortable talking to those friends about things anyway, having had them push me for information about my father's death only about twice in years of friendship. They were more a matter of convenience than anything else.

By the time I'd successfully screwed up my relationships with Josaphine, my sister (because why else would she not feel she could talk to me before bloodying her wrists?), the first Thomas and my friends at school, I decided that I couldn't be trusted. Besides, it took raw *effort* to have people needing you and needing people. I decided that I didn't want that.

In relationships, I was fake. So, it was simple.

'Well,' Colton said, index finger running a line across my arm, 'I reckon I can handle the angry masses driven to madness by me taking you off the public's hands.'

'It's not that,' I said. 'Jacinta's only just out of hospital . . .'

'And?'

'And, bizarrely, we've forged a semi-understanding that I'd rather not shoot to hell quite so soon,' I said. 'And besides, my mother is going to *freak*. People are just going to believe that I'm ignoring my carpinomen. The Thomases of the world are going to be in uproar. They'll try to really push the streaming into farming . . . I just . . . I'd rather not, actually.'

'There's already rumours,' Colton said. 'Lidea saw us having dinner at the Brookes.'

'Then what's with this need for drama?' I asked, pulling myself from under his arm, crossing my legs and turning to face him. 'Why would you want to make me miserable, Colt?'

'I don't,' Colton said, 'but this secret relationship business is trying my patience. You're so self-conscious.'

'Can we just . . . I don't see why you want to storm into school and start kissing. To me, that seems like the worst idea since . . . since my sister thought Brett Jones was quite attractive or my dad decided to drive to work.'

'It's hardly the same,' Colton said.

'Well, no,' I agreed, 'but I still think it's a bad idea.'

'I don't know that we have that much *choice*,' Colton said. 'You do realize the size of Lidea's mouth?'

'Yes,' I said. 'I have nightmares about it *eating* me while I sleep.'

It was true that Lidea had seen Colton and me out for dinner, but that didn't necessarily mean that we were a couple. Although we were. And Lidea would definitely assume that we were, because Lidea loved nothing more than a scandal . . . and this was certainly a scandal.

'How bad can it be?' Colton asked, his expression oddly hopeful.

Colton had never been dragged into the public eye before. I felt like his common name helped with things (there were about four Coltons around our age alone), because if ever he *did* anything there was always a chance that it would be chalked up to someone else. He was attractive, but not overly so. He was running on a par with the average in terms of being streamed (if hanging about in non-specific Further Education a little, but that wasn't very noticeable). His sister was so young that there was no possible way he could be drawn into public attention through her.

At the beginning of last week, if someone had said, 'Oh, guess what, I saw Corin on a date with Colton', the response would have been, 'Which? The tall one? Colton Bridgewater . . . wait, I thought he was the blond one? No? Oh . . .' But when this came to light, everyone in the whole damn Education Centre was going to forget that the blond Colton Bridgewater had ever existed.

'We'll see,' I said primly, dreading it already.

My fringe had snuck up on me, growing to the point where it feathered in front of my vision if I was looking at the wrong angle. I leaned close to the mirror holding the scissors aloft, trying to get access to a straight line. My mother had screamed at me the first time I'd taken a pair of scissors to my hair, cutting the brutal straight fringe that then became my trademark, but the feeling of empowerment was worth the backlash.

I had a ruler somewhere in my room although I wasn't entirely sure where, so I was simply aiming for something vaguely straight.

'Corin,' Jacinta said, slamming open the door and causing me to slip mid-snip.

'What are you *doing*?' I demanded, holding the scissors and feeling slightly in shock. 'Jacinta,' I said. 'Jacinta, what have you *done*?'

Although ruler-straight wasn't a strict criteria, I certainly hadn't been aiming for having *a chunk missing from my fringe*.

'Serves you right for playing hairdresser without adequate training,' Jacinta said, eyes darting towards the gap in my hair. The corners of her lips tilted upwards slightly.

'You . . .' I began, wordless rage stirring up in my gut as I glanced back at the mirror. It would grow back. I knew it wasn't *really* Jacinta's fault any more than it wasn't really my fault, but the damage was done.

'It doesn't look much more ridiculous than normal,'

Jacinta said, still as snide as ever. 'Anyway, we're going to be late.'

'Yes,' I said, dropping the scissors in the sink and narrowing my eyes at her, 'because your dramatic entrance *massacred* my hair.'

'Please,' Jacinta said, glancing up at my fringe again, 'no one will even notice the difference.'

'I'm driving.'

'No,' Jacinta said, running the keys through her finger. 'I want to drive.'

'You *hate* driving,' I muttered, taking the stairs two at a time and bursting out onto the street, 'and it's *my* car.'

'Pity you don't have insurance,' Jacinta said, her voice twisting with malice.

Yes, we had almost reached an impasse where we *tried* to be slightly understanding of each other's point of view since the night in the hospital, but that didn't mean we'd fundamentally changed who we were. And, fundamentally, we were two sisters who drove each other *mental*.

It might have been nice not to argue with her for once, but I simply didn't know how.

'*Your* fault,' I spat, staring as my sister took the driving seat. I did not like my sister driving. 'Pretty sure you shouldn't be driving with all those meds in you,' I added, 'not least because you'll start to *rattle* if you brake too hard.'

'No chance of that if you were driving,' Jacinta said, 'given you don't seem to have any knowledge of what a brake is or does.'

'I'll break you.'

'Please.'

'Those drugs are making you *far* too responsive,' I commented, dragging out my TTC and messaging Colton (who was mildly annoyed that I was opting to ride with Jacinta, rather than dragging him to our road to give me a lift — apparently there was something wrong with me not giving him my time during Education Centre hours *and* on the way there). 'I preferred the ones that made you shut up.'

'Sorry, Corin,' Jacinta said, glancing over in my direction, 'I can't take you seriously with your hair that uneven. Why didn't you try and cut it straight?'

I swore at her, irritation flaring up in a hot burst of *wanting to strangle her* before I managed to squash it down slightly. Why was she such a pain in the arse? She couldn't just *shut up* and stop trying to interfere with my life. She just *had* to throw open the door while I was cutting my hair. She just *had* to ruin everything.

'They're streaming me,' Jacinta said, after a few minutes.

'What?' I demanded. 'What to? What the hell are you useful for?'

'Engineering,' Jacinta returned, her voice cool.

'How the hell are you more emotionally stable than me?' I demanded, staring at her. 'You've only just been let out of *mental* hospital, so why are they leaving me to rot in this godforsaken building while even *you* manage to get out?'

'I thought,' Jacinta said, 'you could attempt to be *pleased*.'

'Why?' I asked, sending another — slightly angrier — message to Colton from my TTC.

Jacinta turned her sharpest gaze at me before focusing on the road.

Well.

When we pulled into the car park, Colton was already there, dawdling by his car to waste the few minutes until I arrived. I had been planning on chastising him for waiting for me (which I'd known he'd do, from his messages), but I was so riled up and *angry* at everything that I suddenly wanted the scandal.

The government couldn't tell me what to do. They had no right to tell me what I could do with my life and what I couldn't. They didn't have the power to stop me from kissing whoever I wanted whenever they wanted. They could choose my life's direction and purpose, or treat the Education Centre like a holding pen and leave me there until my flesh started to rot off my bones, but they couldn't touch the things I *thought* or *felt.*

'Hey,' I said, slamming the door of my car behind me as I strode up to Colton, grabbed his hand and pulled him into a clumsy kiss.

Colton hadn't been expecting it, obviously, but neither had anyone else in the car park. The silence was just about deafening and, in unison, everyone in the whole place seemed to have directed their gaze towards us.

'Morning,' Colton said, drawing back and raising an eyebrow at me. 'Corin, what the bloody hell have you done to your hair?'

This was by far the worst it had ever been.

It had gone beyond the point where I suspected everyone in the Education Centre knew my name (a thought that was now a dead cert rather than paranoia, after the day I'd had), but I was now half convinced that my name would be etched onto the walls of the toilets and handed down to all their great-grandchildren.

Corin Blacksmith: the girl who dated.

'What does she think she's doing?' Lidea Crackmore asked from the seat in front, a sense of extreme déjà vu settling over me.

'Colton Furnish,' I interjected loudly.

'What?' Jenny asked.

'That's what I'm doing,' I said, adding a friendly smile for good measure. Jenny's complexion coloured dramatically and the silence thickened. Suddenly the air in the Education Centre was *dense* with the atmosphere of a couple of hundred judging students.

Jenny and Lidea turned back to the front and to each other.

'The broken heart must have got to her,' Lidea finally concluded, in another of her loud whispers. 'I expect Tom feels awful.'

'Sorry,' I said, tapping her on the shoulder, 'which Tom are you talking about? It'd be nice to know, for context, which Tom you're actually talking about here.'

It was hard not to laugh directly in their faces.

'Tom Asquith,' Jenny breathed, seemingly unable to leave a question unanswered.

'Right,' I said, nodding. 'OK, thanks.'

'She's going the same way as her sister,' Lidea said, pausing as if to allow me a second to interject. I didn't. I could reel off smarmy comments about myself, and about the various Thomases, and about Colton Furnish, but my sister remained an issue that should stay undiscussed. '*Crazy*,' Lidea added, tapping her forehead. 'Just look at her hair.'

'Hair isn't indicative of your mental state,' I said in my normal voice – cutting across the teacher's explanation about enzymes and glaring at the back of Lidea's neck. 'If it were, I assume that your choice of colour might have got you sectioned. I do worry about the state of your sanity though; given that you appear to have a *remarkable* disregard for your own health or wellbeing.'

'What?'

'Well, unless you were purposefully trying to damage yourself I fail to see why you'd bring my sister into this.'

'Stop *eavesdropping*–'

'Then find something more interesting to talk about than my life. You could, you know, try having one of your own.'

'We're not all *like you*, Corin,' Lidea said, turning her whole body round in her chair and *glaring* at me. There was nothing actually wrong with Lidea. Apart from the fact that she was a tremendous gossip with a loud voice she was actually quite nice, but I wasn't in the mood to be forgiving – I wanted a fight.

'Obviously not,' I said. 'I have a working volume switch. It's helpful. It means if I were to talk about your *questionable* liaisons with Cris Bennett no one else would hear about it.'

Her face turned white.

'Oh, *whoops*, I guess I forgot to press the mute button. *Silly me.*'

'That's not true,' Lidea muttered. 'You're making it up.'

'I doubt it matters whether it's true or not,' I said, 'as people will still talk. Loudly. Right in front of you. *Enjoy it, Lidea.*'

I had expected that Jacinta would choose our home to be the backdrop to the inevitable scene where she told me exactly what she thought of my latest terrible decision, but in actual fact it took place shortly after my third lesson of the day.

One second I was walking towards my next classroom and the next, Jacinta had an iron-tight grip round my arm and was dragging me towards a corner of the corridor.

Out of the two of us, I was the violent one. I was the one who did things without thinking of the consequences because of what I felt in the moment. I was much more likely to cause bruises if someone pissed me off, while Jacinta was softer and calmer (unless in the middle of one of her episodes, when she was nearly a different person anyway).

'What the hell are you doing?' Jacinta asked.

Her nails were digging into my skin through my clothes. It hurt.

'I don't think it has anything to do with you,' I said curtly, trying to pull my arm out of her grasp.

'Really?' Jacinta demanded, her voice low.

'Yes.'

'You're my *sister*.'

'And you forfeited the right to have any say over my life *years* ago,' I said, squaring my arms and glaring at her.

'Why are you doing this?'

'You don't know the half of it,' I said, lips twisting. 'This doesn't concern you.'

'I *will* stop you.'

'What are you going to do?' I asked. 'Tell Mum?'

'If I have to,' Jacinta said.

'I am not under anyone's control.'

'You certainly have no *self-control*,' Jacinta spat. 'Is that what this is about?'

'Sex?' I questioned. 'No, it isn't. Thank you, once again, for the glowing character assessment. And you wonder why I don't listen to you?'

'This will ruin you,' Jacinta said, her grip finally slackening on my arm. I took a purposeful step back and away from her, briefly reminded that only three weeks ago we'd been having an actual conversation about our *feelings*. I wondered how she'd feel knowing that I'd already been in this relationship with Colton back then. I imagined it wouldn't make her mood much better.

'No,' I said, 'life ruined me. Dad ruined me. You ruined me. Mum ruined me. *This* is me taking control of my ruin and doing *what I want*.'

'You don't know what you want,' Jacinta said. 'You don't know what you're *doing*. Why can't you just be *careful*?'

'This conversation is over,' I said, taking another step backwards. 'I don't want anything to do with you, Jacinta.'

I turned away, shaking slightly with a lethal cocktail of

indignation, rage and the desire to run away and hide from anything and everything. Jacinta made me tired. She emotionally drained me *all* the time and it was so difficult to deal with.

I didn't want to deal with it.

'I don't want anything to do with a girl prepared to be in a non-anima-vinculum relationship.'

I turned round.

'Bit rich coming from you,' I said, closing the space between us slightly, 'but the thing is, Jacinta, *I've been doing it for years*.'

And with the satisfying sense of the drama of the situation ringing through my brain, I turned round once more and walked off down the corridor (trying to ignore the ghost of the pain that lingered around the place where Jacinta had grabbed me).

'Oi, Blacksmith!'

Thomas Grit arrived in the corridor, nudging me with his arm and raising a pair of aggressively dark eyebrows at me.

'Did you want anything in particular?'

'You could have picked me instead of Colt,' Thomas said, puffing out his chest with a grin, 'although I gotta admit this is more dramatic.'

'Yes,' I agreed. 'Obviously that's why I'm doing it. I aim for drama in all walks of life.'

'If you ever want another Thomas . . .' Grit said, saluting before disappearing off to some distant direction of the dining hall. He probably didn't want to be seen entering the lion's den with me, which I could well understand, but I really wished that I didn't have to do *this* alone.

Occasionally, I got that uncomfortable prickle at the back of my neck that convinced me that I was being watched . . . but that was nothing compared to the concrete knowledge that *everyone* with this lunch period in the Education Centre was looking at me.

Colton hadn't answered my messages for the past thirty minutes. While I knew he'd been in a class at this point, I would have expected a smarmy comment or two, or at least something from him to reassure me when he'd be arriving for lunch.

I was not insecure, but considering he was the one who wanted *this publicity* it hardly seemed fair to strand me in the middle of it.

'Josa,' I said, acknowledging the girl stiffly before falling into one of the empty seats.

We rarely spoke, Josaphine and I, instead occasionally meeting each other's eyes and awkwardly looking away (the same thing I did whenever I saw Tom Asquith too, because I couldn't look at him without seeing his wrist), but there were barely enough seats in the dining hall as it was.

She looked good. Her skin had always been better than mine, her features more classically attractive, and much more refined and *sweet*. These days, she'd turned from cute little child into something nearing beautiful.

'Corin,' Josaphine said, her voice heavier than normal. 'Having a good day?' she added shrewdly, glancing around at the rest of the hall with a small smile.

Everyone was staring. At me.

'Wonderful,' I returned tersely.

'I wonder,' Josaphine asked. 'Are you planning on running through the whole list of popular boys' names, or just the top three?'

'What's the third?'

'Jak,' Josaphine said, her lips tilting up slightly.

'No attractive ones that spring to mind,' I said, digging out my lunch from my bag, 'although Colton's father ... No, I imagine that might irritate Colton a bit, so I might stick with the first two.'

'And so the mystery continues.'

'Not for you,' I said.

She looked up and her eyes met mine. Dark brown, familiar, unblinking. Josaphine was the single person in the world who had seen my wrist, and she'd let me serial date Thomases without feeling the need to comment or judge ... and now she was letting my relationship with Colton slip by too. She wasn't judgemental. She didn't feel the need to categorize people like the rest of the world did.

Sometimes I really missed Josaphine.

'Guess not,' Josaphine agreed, before looking back down at her tabloid and scrolling through something — probably a conversation with someone. It seemed like I'd stumbled across her in the middle of something ... but Josaphine was always up to something or other.

'Hey,' Colton said, sitting down in the seat next to me with a distinct grin. Josaphine looked up from her TTC for a split second, but by then my attention had been eclipsed by the frankly *alarmingly* happy expression that seemed to radiate from Colton.

'You didn't answer my messages,' I said, glancing up at him and frowning.

'Wow, needy.' Colton grinned, nudging me with his elbow. 'Sorry, they called me out of class for a meeting with my streamer.'

'Oh?'

'I'm starting at the University Centre next week.'

'What?' I asked, sitting up a little straighter. 'For literary sciences, like you wanted?'

'Yep,' Colton said, his face practically glowing with the joy of it. 'This is the bit where you could pretend to be happy with me.'

'Yeah,' I said, 'give me a minute to work up some real *joy*.'

They were trying to contain the situation. Obviously, my friendship – now relationship – with Colton *was* the reason why I'd suddenly been streamed into farming and why, after months of being told it wasn't possible, Colton was landing his dream career. I'd assumed that it was something to do with Colton being an immanis and me being a general trouble-causer, so they were punishing us for mixing . . . but Colton was getting his dream career handed to him on a plate.

Even *Jacinta* was getting streamed upwards.

My life was stagnant and fruitless. My high grades got me nothing but further enlistment in more barely interesting classes. If they wanted to drive me and Colton away from each other, why the hell couldn't *I* be the one streamed elsewhere? Anywhere that *wasn't* farming?

'Corin,' Colton said, sounding genuinely hurt, 'this is my *dream*.'

'Yes, congratulations,' I said, staring at the dining table.

'Fine,' Colton said. 'Don't be pleased.'

'Don't get self-righteous with me, Colt,' I muttered. 'Of course I'm pleased. I just think it's a bit coincidental.'

'In what way?'

I gave him a look.

'If you're talking about your *magnificent* display in the car park this morning, then that's hardly my fault. You could have *said* you were going to out us. It would have been nice to have been prepared, rather than stuck in the middle of a plot to stick a metaphorical middle finger up at your sister.'

'Stop *nagging* me about it,' I returned heatedly. 'God, Colt. You're impossible.'

'*I'm* impossible?' Colton questioned, leaning forward slightly. 'Corin, do you ever *look* at your behaviour?'

'Yes,' I said, squaring up my shoulders and glaring at him. 'I look at my behaviour, I look at my life, I look at *everything* and I wonder why the *hell* everyone else gets exactly what they want, while I just have to deal with what life gives me.'

'So you're in a bad mood,' Colton commented.

'Congratulations,' I said. 'Are you sure literature is your calling? Maybe you should try *detecting*.'

'I'm *detecting* that whatever I say is going to be wrong right now,' Colton said, 'but given that the whole school is *watching us*, maybe it might be an idea for you to at least *pretend* you like me.'

'I'm not that good an actor.'

'Could have fooled me.'

'I have,' I said, reaching out for his hand and threading my fingers through his, 'repeatedly. Sorry, I'm being . . . unreasonable.'

'It's fine,' Colton said, shrugging slightly. 'You're unreasonable most of the time.'

'Oi,' I said, rolling my eyes and picking up my fork again. 'Well, I guess I no longer have a lift to the Education Centre.'

'Jacinta?' Colton suggested.

'I very much doubt she'll allow me to share her oxygen for a while, let alone the same car,' I said. 'Colton, why is everyone in the whole world so annoying?'

'Am I annoying?'

'Yes,' I said, 'very. It's a good job you're attractive.'

'Thanks,' Colton said. 'You're right, though. I have quite literally got *everything* I have ever wanted.'

'Spare me,' I said, resting my forehead on his shoulder for a second, 'and if you so much as *think* of writing me a poem I'm going to cut off your thumb and steal your car. OK?'

'Got it,' Colton said, pressing a kiss onto the top of my head for a split second. 'Sorry you're having a bad day.'

'I'd say it's not your fault,' I muttered into the material of his jacket, 'but it actually is.'

'Want to come over later?'

'Definitely,' I said, dragging myself from the security of Colton's shoulder and staring, drained, at my food.

A number of people in the room were still staring at us, but it was only as I returned to my lunch that I caught Josaphine's eye and realized that she was staring at the pair of us too.

Maybe she wasn't as accepting as I had previously thought.

13

The Cynicism Movement

Colton's face flickered into focus on the screen in front of me. His eyes didn't have that same absorbent quality via the screen, but then I didn't really have a choice in the matter any more. Face-to-face chat via tabloids was better than the on-going silence of the past few days, even if it was a long way off the hug I wanted.

I was falling into a routine of relying on Colton for some degree of social support, which was strange. I'd become really rather good at being self-sufficient and being on my own, so this new reset to factory settings and *needing* people was an uncomfortable feeling to carry around all day.

'Hey,' I said, waving and pulling my seat closer to the screen.

'How bad is it?' Colton asked, his voice not quite lining up with his mouth movements. Jacinta had got the room with the better connection to the internet, while my room was at the back of the house. I got a view of the garden.

I grimaced. 'Well, I'm never allowed to leave the house ever again, except for the Education Centre and work.'

'So it's even more draconian than it was yesterday?'

'Yep,' I said. Yesterday the instructions were that I wasn't allowed to leave the house with any *male* individual ever again. 'I made a lot of lesbian comments.'

'Right,' Colton laughed.

I could see snatches of his bedroom behind him and felt an immense desire to sneak out my bedroom window and walk to his house. It wasn't even that *far*, but with the threats my mother was making it probably wasn't worth it. Yesterday, she'd threatened to tell the government that I was the mystery farmer in the family and have me shipped off to the countryside with a chastity belt and a spare pair of wellingtons. The woman was madder than I'd ever seen her.

'I told you it was a bad idea,' I told Colton, folding my arms, 'and you insisted because you're an idiot who couldn't accept I liked you unless the *whole world* knew.'

'Well, were you expecting the reaction to be quite so . . . ?'

'Volcanic?' I asked, grimacing. 'Not really. I knew it was going to be bad, but I didn't realize we were going to revert to pre-teen *grounding*.'

'Well,' Colton said, 'at least you're allowed to go to the Education Centre.'

'That's my silver lining?' I asked. 'Colt, that's muddy grey at best. That's probably the darkest, wettest part of the whole cloud, actually. Why did you have to go and be all successful? How is your degree going?'

'Corin, I've only been here two days.'

'Feels like a lifetime to me.' I frowned. 'Wanting people to be around is rubbish. Why did Jacinta have to tell Mum everything?'

Not only was I being punished for one non-anima-vinculum boyfriend, I was also being punished for each individual Thomas past. Telling Jacinta my carpinomen wasn't Thomas might have felt satisfying at the time, but it turned out not to have been one of the best decisions I'd ever made.

Still, it was going to have to have happened at some point. Assuming I conceded and ended up with my carpinomen, of course.

'It is a bit ironic,' Colton said, shrugging slightly on the screen, 'but still, look on the bright side — we're practically Romeo and Juliet.'

'Can we make a *not* committing suicide pact?' I suggested. 'I don't really want your death on my hands. Or my own.'

'Sure,' Colton said. 'Maybe I could come see you while you're at work?'

'I'm waitressing,' I said with a grimace. 'You'd have to book into a meal there and hope I ended up serving your table. I wouldn't really be able to talk to you.'

One of the few things I liked about the government education system was their attitude to non-skilled work. As soon as you hit Level Three courses, you were assigned a part-time job — one full day at some point on your assigned weekend, then one evening a week. They paid you a minimal amount which provided every teenager with a base income for clothes, entertaining themselves, perhaps setting up a car fund . . . while filling up all the unskilled jobs so that it wasn't *necessary* for adults to work in those jobs. I preferred waitressing to any of the other jobs I'd been assigned over the years and, obviously trying to appease my anger a little, Mary Cuttleworth had kept me at the same restaurant since I turned fifteen.

You could give up your job the second you were streamed into Further Education, keep it until you found yourself streamed into an actual career or, after completing a full Level Three course, choose to take on your job full-time and give up education (they gave you a chance to come back to it at any time too).

'I'll pick you up after work?' Colton suggested. 'We can run into the sunset and leave this small world behind us.'

'My mother has arranged transport,' I said. 'Apparently she resented me telling her I *had* to date you because, while Jacinta was in hospital, I had no other way of getting places. Grig next door has just passed his driving test, so Mum's hiring him to chauffeur me around as from tomorrow.'

'I thought you weren't supposed to talk to anyone male ever again?'

'I said that,' I admitted. 'Mum seemed to think, because he's sixteen, he's probably safe from my lusty fingers.'

'Is he? Should I be jealous?'

'Ha ha,' I said, putting my legs up on my desk and watching Colton for a few seconds. 'I very much doubt I'll be allowed to drive my car again till I've left home. I might sell it to spite Jacinta.'

'Is there anything you wouldn't do to spite Jacinta?' Colton grinned.

'At the moment, no,' I admitted, 'but then we are a family in the grip of desperation. I think my mother would confiscate my tabloid if it wasn't illegal.'

'Bless the law,' Colton said. 'Where would we be then?'

'In the same place as we are now,' I returned sarcastically. 'Just unable to communicate through this lovely screen. Are you OK? How's Ava? I suppose your parents haven't flipped out.'

'Ava's good,' Colton said, grinning, 'and no, they haven't. But, then again, I haven't serial-dated lots of girls called Becky or whatever.'

'Well, they could hardly talk anyway,' I said, wrapping my arms around myself and frowning at the computer screen. 'This wouldn't be such a big deal if it wasn't for Jacinta's big reaction to Brett. I don't remember *her* being grounded.'

'Just hospitalized.'

'Exactly!' I said. 'Eurgh, never mind. Have you read any more of the books I downloaded for you?' I dropped my voice slightly, mindful that my mother – diligent for the sake of my dignity as always – might possibly be standing outside my door, eavesdropping. Well, she was sure to be quite disappointed; I wasn't about to start spouting sordid comments about our relationship, or drippy declaratives about how much I missed him.

Even though I did miss him. A lot more than I'd probably expected.

Then again, Mum was only talking to me to tell me I was an idiot and Jacinta was communicating purely through the medium of death glares. Everyone at school seemed unsure whether to treat me as though I had some sort of contagious disease, or to continually harass me for details about my relationship with Thomases/Colton or else Colton's sudden disappearance to the University Centre.

'I'm partway through the one about the miserable French people,' Colton said, 'although I'm finding it difficult to read.'

'Because it's dry and long-winded?'

'No,' Colton said. 'Although he's certainly not rationing words or back story. I meant . . . the font. Corin, that's the font your TTC's all in, isn't it? Where do I recognize it from?'

My heart sped up slightly and I pulled my chair closer towards the screen. This was important. Of all the, admittedly subtle, hints I'd been dropping this was one of the last I'd expected him to pick up on . . . there was this possibility — although it was very slim — that Colton might be intelligent enough to spot the same things I had while reading those books.

He was doing a degree for goodness' sake. Hardly *anyone* did a degree these days. Undeniably one of the reasons they'd let him was because they were trying to drive a physical wedge between us, but he was still *capable* of the thing.

'It's . . . I'm surprised you recognize it,' I said, leaning forward and dropping my voice further. 'It's . . . it's called wrist font.'

'Wrist font?' Colton questioned, the volume of his voice making me wince slightly. *Wrist font* was not something that was supposed to be talked about in anything more than whispers, preferably not mentioned at all and just *noticed*.

'It's a mock-up of . . . of carpinomen,' I said, my throat feeling unconsciously tight. 'It's . . .'

'Ah,' Colton said, reaching out and typing something, 'it's difficult to read.'

'Well, it wasn't meant for screens.'

'But skin,' Colton said, 'so someone must have sat and . . . looked at lots of carpinomens and mocked up a font?'

'That,' I said, 'or their carpinomen had a very long name.'

A message came through. I opened the tab. Colton.

He'd typed *Corin* in wrist font. I stared at it for a few moments, my heart speeding up slightly in my chest. I'd never written my name out in it before. It had never occurred to me to do so. Yet this is what my name would look like on someone else's wrist . . . there were only about a hundred people in the country whose wrist had *that* on it.

'Why were you surprised I didn't recognize it?' Colton asked.

'If you've only had the one name to reference from . . .' I said, trailing off. I'd seen two wrists in my lifetime, but then I'd stumbled across wrist font and used it for just about everything *because* it was so horrifying and fascinating that I couldn't look away.

'I've seen my parents' wrists,' Colton said.

'What?'

'I mean . . . I didn't believe them, for ages, when they told me that they weren't . . . weren't soul mates.'

'So they got their wrists out?'

'Yeah,' Colton said, shrugging his shoulders, 'and they're right. They're not soul mates. That's still only a few more letters, though . . . where did you get this font from?'

'Contacts,' I said, running the word round my mouth a few times. It tasted slightly sour. It was such a go-to response whenever Colton asked too much. Sometimes I felt like if I was able to push myself further to tell him *more* then he'd instantly pick up on more . . . maybe, then, we'd get somewhere.

Colton, I typed back in wrist font, just because it seemed like the only adequate written reply I could give. Colton's name looked a little too good in wrist font and I didn't want to think about that much either.

'Have you got a contact for everything?'

'That's the idea,' I said. 'Look, Colt, I've got some homework to do. Message me later?'

'OK,' Colton said. 'Try not to piss off your mum too much. I'd like to actually see you at some point before I die.'

'Don't count on it,' I said, waving for a split second before I shut the conversation down and took a deep breath.

I needed to get up and walk around. I needed to *move* and get out of the house. My assigned weekend had been changed (probably another movement from the higher-ups) and I was beginning to feel a little stir-crazy. I'd been driven to school by Jacinta, who was still working on Additional mathematics for engineers in the Further Education Block for another two weeks, and then been hunted by the gossips and busybodies for *hours* before being driven straight back home. The car journeys had been long, arduous affairs where Jacinta — whose confidence seemed to have been knocked slightly — drove much too slowly, looking continually terrified, and refused to talk to me.

I couldn't face going downstairs and running into my mother, but if I stayed in my room for another minute then I was going to explode and seriously damage something (probably my tabloid). The bathroom was, depressingly, the only other option I had left to me.

Well, it would do.

I had a quick shower, more for something to do than anything else, and felt slightly better for it.

I hadn't exactly been lying to Colton about having homework but I had absolutely no intention of doing any of it and was instead planning to flirt something interesting out of Ean, or else look back over that footage of the D'livere (because I'd barely heard about that for months . . . and I'd been expecting something to happen to the ridiculous monument).

With one of the bright blue towels wrapped around myself, I stepped back out into the corridor and walked across to my room. I froze in the doorway, dumbstruck, as the horror of the thing settled over my chest.

Jacinta was in my room. Worse, she was sitting at the chair in front of my tabloid *staring* at my screen.

There were plenty of things she could have found on my

tabloid that would induce that expression of horror: aeons of files saved under the name of various classes, numerous clips of teenagers trying to kill themselves, details of government screw-ups and the subsequent cover-ups, wrist font – a whole history of things I'd thought about hidden in the dustier parts of my tabloid.

Oh my God.

Jacinta . . . Jacinta *knew*. The knowledge was written all over her face, which meant, whatever she'd found, she'd put enough pieces together to come to the conclusion – Corin Blacksmith was a member of the cynicism movement.

Let me get this straight.

I had never intended to be involved in the movement. I wasn't looking to turn into a political outcast.

Dad was dead, Jacinta wanted to be dead and the first Thomas turned out to be just as much of an arse as I'd expected him to be. And so I started searching for *something* to take my mind off these things. I found my contact. I found that I could get inside access to the news and traced out the discrepancies between the truth and what we were allowed to know. Sometimes, there were just a few differences in semantics – a word or two substituted, revealing a subtle difference that meant so much – and sometimes there were whole sides of stories obliterated from public knowledge and left to rot unknown and unexplained.

I started to wonder. I dug deeper. I found that there was a whole host of banned books.

First, I fell in love with this massive database of stories and characters. I didn't care so much about myself when I could immerse myself in other people's problems (not real-life people who could *depend* on you and *expect* something from you, but these people who you could be emotionally invested in without ever having a conversation with them). But then there were the questions. Why was it that in all these years of literature, in Shakespeare, in the stories and poems of the Brontë sisters, in Tolkien, in Harry Potter, that *no one* had a carpinomen?

At school, they sold you this fairy story about Greek mythology. The age of the thing always seemed to shock me, because it was thousands and thousands of years before anyone had even thought about my existence, and yet people still had another half of their soul that they were to search for. Except, all the other novels that they allowed you to read (there were a few) seemed to have no carpinomen. They sold this to you as an ancient convention of literature, but by the time I'd studied Level Four linguistics I could tell the difference in time between extracts of Shakespeare and extracts of *The Secret Garden* . . . and then I went on to study O&E and all the other bits of things about English that seemed to imply a lot more than the Education Centre seemed to realize.

So, I had this unrelenting craving to know more. And I had these huge questions pressing at the back of my brain, all the time, while the world pushed in with these problems that I didn't want to deal with (because people were talking about Jacinta at school, and they were dragging my name through the mud thanks to all the business with Thomas and my mum wasn't OK and it *hurt*) . . . so I went searching for the truth.

What I found was the cynicism movement.

It was one of those things that everyone was aware of, but was more of a joke than a legitimate thing. If someone was being particularly unrealistic in their views, you might ask to see their membership to the cynics. There were political activists around the school — the eco kids who told you off for driving your car, the naturalists who insisted on eating actual *flesh* rather than the reconstructed meat, but you never saw the cynics.

Never.

I'd never met one. My only experience of them was the glimpses on TV, which were designed to perpetuate their image as complete lunatics (which the TV companies managed, of course).

It took a long time to find them. First I found the wrist font, then I found a conspiracy theorist who believed that no one actually had a name on their wrist (I quickly wrote that off after a quick glance at my wrist, because *yes*, the name was still there), but that led on to another person who believed that the carpinomen phenomenon was all a damn lie.

And there it was.

I wanted to hate the idea of soul mates anyway, because already I felt horrified that I had no *choice* but to follow this predesigned life path just because there was this apparent piece of my 'soul' that was connected to another individual. I wanted to hate the idea of soul mates because it meant my mother was going to stay alone until the day she died. The idea of soul mates clashed so terribly with how my sister falling in love had nearly resulted in her death. I didn't *want* this name on my wrist to define who I was.

Besides, the cynics made sense. There was stuff that no

one had ever been able to explain to me. What genetic advantage did a carpinomen give us? How did it even happen? Why were we not born with the name on our wrists? How come everyone I had asked had visited a hospital only once (coincidentally just before their carpinomen appeared, although they only surrendered this information when really pressed or asked indirectly)?

I stopped believing in the whole damn stupid convention, wound up spending my whole life finding further proof for my theory, following the dark, gritty side of the lies and trying to find some *answer* as to why the government would brand names onto skin and try to sell us some romantic story about our souls.

I'd wanted Colton to question these things. I'd wanted him to *prove* that I wasn't the only person in the world who could see through them.

I took another step further into the room.

My tabloid was open on a conversation with one of the other cynics I'd stumbled into online. He thought I was a thirty-two-year-old gay man, but then I doubted very much that he was a science teacher in Mexico . . . it didn't matter, though. It hadn't been a social conversation. He'd been whining about how *blind* everyone was to the blatant truth of it all . . . drawing on everyday explicit examples that no one noticed, ranting on and on about how frustrated he was that no one could see properly.

I hadn't read the latest messages because Colton had wanted to talk, but there was bound to be enough information to damn me.

Jacinta was staring at the screen with her eyes wide.

Being a cynic wasn't illegal, but there had to be a reason why you never saw them. They disappeared. Cryptic messages advising *Don't talk to me again* left me questioning whether I was being paranoid, or if I was just talking to teenage girls trying to mock a bunch of crazies, or if maybe they just gave up fighting the impossible and went to search for the one they were doomed to spend an eternity with.

'What are you doing?' I asked, slightly breathless.

It was a turn-up for the books that she'd now think I was the one who was crazy, when she was the nut job with the robotic state and the episodes.

Jacinta wasn't breathing.

I hoped to hell she hadn't watched any of the video clips of the suicides. I didn't want my perverse obsession with watching what fellow cynics would do to trigger my sister into another breakdown (having watched a live version of the wrist-slitting routine, the grainy footage I had access to was nothing), but I also didn't want her to think my desire to watch such clips had come from her *own* actions.

Most of all, I wanted her not to have seen anything on my tabloid.

Jacinta opened her mouth but didn't seem able to speak. My head was spinning. We were both frozen in the moment, stagnant with the shock of it.

Oh my God.

Jacinta knew.

Jacinta knew that I was a cynic. I hated people knowing things about me. I hated people being able to *hurt* me with things, and suddenly my sister was acutely aware of the one secret I had managed to keep from her for years. *She knew*.

'Get out of my room,' I said, my voice dropping slightly.

She didn't need telling twice. She suddenly burst into movement — reminding me acutely of when she was on the drugs — as if she couldn't get out of the room fast enough. She was falling, falling towards the door and past me and out into the corridor.

'Sorry,' Jacinta muttered, barely out loud.

'Fine,' I said, my face burning.

I stepped into my room, shutting the door behind me. My legs were taking me towards my tabloid; I fell into my seat, facing the conversation that Jacinta had read.

I've got to go, I typed out to the other cynic, before I deleted the entire conversation history.

The systematic deletion of four years of hard flirting should have hurt, but my brain had skipped over to automatic: the video clips, the novels, the old movies, the saved conversations, the obscure articles, the blog posts, the wrist font, the aliases I'd made up along the way . . .

It wasn't safe if Jacinta knew. I couldn't have the evidence left on my tabloid any longer. I couldn't be that vulnerable.

Maybe that's why the other cynics disappeared. No wild government intervention or dramatic standoffs, just someone walking in at the wrong moment and seeing something that made them a subject of ridicule.

For years I'd been assuming that my tabloid was secure and, more than anything, I was filled with the awareness that if I'd just locked my tabloid before climbing into the shower then none of this would have ever happened. Jacinta would have been stuck on the lock screen. She'd never have been able to dig into my life and come up with a *diamond* secret that was sure to be my ruin.

I hadn't even registered my grip on the towel had slipped, my bare flesh uncovered, modesty forgotten.

I had no idea what Jacinta would do with this information.

Pulling the towel upwards to cover my breasts again, I stared down at my knees and realized with a jolt that I'd just deleted several years of my life off my hard drive. Mostly I just felt an all-consuming exhaustion, but there was some small part of me that very much wanted to cry.

14

Escape

'So, everyone had a good day?' I asked, glancing up at my mum and my sister.

Meal times had become a silent vigil, punctuated only by the odd irritated comment sent from one direction or another. If I'd known total destruction of the family unit could be completely secured by a little name-dropping (or at least, non-carpinomen name-dropping) than I might have done it before. I did so *love* flaring up their irritation.

Except, honestly, this was wearing a little thin.

'Fine,' Mum said, stabbing her potato a little too violently.

'Good,' I said. 'I had a great day too,' I continued. 'They tried to stream me into farming again. I said I'd stage a mass protest. Oddly I think Mary Cuttleworth is actually a little scared. Apparently the higher-ups think I have enough public influence to actually start something.'

I hadn't had a great day. Colton was apparently much too interested in his degree to message me, which I could completely understand given it was actually quite exciting and important for his future . . . I hated to be needy and all, but I detested suddenly being cut off and left to deal with the Education Centre alone.

I'd found Josaphine staring at me on far too many occasions, which was mildly more disturbing than facing Lidea or Tom Asquith (who seemed to be everywhere lately) and didn't help with my shot nerves. I did not *want* to be the talking point of the whole centre, to have people on my back all day, to come home to a place where I wasn't allowed to leave and where no one wanted to talk to me.

'I'm so glad I don't have to leave the house,' I said. 'It's so much *pressure*, you know, to leave . . . and be outside . . . and go places. I'm glad I don't have to deal with that any more.'

'Stop it, Corin,' Mum said, setting down her fork and glaring at me.

'Or what?' I asked. 'Got any more threats?'

'Corin Blacksmith—'

'You gonna keep me hostage till I go searching?'

'I hadn't realized searching was in your plan,' Mum said tightly, 'or were you simply planning on ditching your latest the second they streamed you?'

'I was planning on searching *for myself*,' I said. 'Paris, Rome, Prague, the American Section, the Asian Section.

There's a whole wide world out there. Colton can come with me if he wants.'

'Stop arguing,' Jacinta said quietly.

'Or what? All we ever *do* is argue. It's a family tradition.'

'Corin,' Mum said, her eyes (exact carbon copies of mine, cold blue-grey; one of the few things I'd actually inherited from my mother) flashing a warning that I had no intention of heeding, 'are you aiming to be insolent?'

'You're aiming for annoying,' I retorted.

'I am *aiming* to retain some sense of discipline in this house.'

'Why don't you just lock me up?'

'You're being melodramatic.'

'Yes,' I said, 'I'm making a point. I didn't realize you were a dictator.'

'You're acting like a child.'

'Because you're not letting me be an adult!' I said, slamming down my own cutlery. 'If you'd said, "Let's sit down and have a mature conversation where I value your thoughts and opinions", then maybe I wouldn't have to resort to sass. I'm reacting to what you're giving me, Mum.'

'Really?' Mum asked, standing up and taking my plate from me.

'I wasn't finished.'

'Yes you were.' She walked over to the kitchen and practically threw both our plates at the sink. I vaguely wondered whether she'd broken anything. I hoped she had. At least that way she'd have to spend some of her wages on replacement crockery and

I'd feel slightly vindicated by the whole situation.

'Technically,' I said, kicking my feet out, 'this is starvation.'

'Start making adult decisions if you want to be treated like an adult,' Mum said. 'It's a two-way street, Corin, and I am not willing to allow you to mess up your life.'

'But it's *my* life,' I said. 'That's the point, Mum. It doesn't *belong* to you. You have no *rights* over it.'

'I brought you up.'

'Yes,' I said. 'Thank you, but if I hadn't exerted my free will from the moment of my birth till now, I'd currently be digging up manure. I'd rather not deal with any sort of shit, ta.'

'This conversation is over.'

'It's hardly a conversation,' I said, standing up and kicking my chair back under the table. 'This is purgatory. Thank you, Mum, for making us both miserable. I'm sure you're very proud.'

Jacinta was still hunched over her dinner. At some point she'd switched over to her robotic state without either Mum or me noticing. I felt a small pang of regret at that, because Mum rarely saw Jacinta like this — usually, when we were at home, Jacinta and I bickered and Mum got angry at the two of us bickering.

We *did* always argue; it just wasn't like this.

I had to walk past the pictures in the hallway to storm up to my room. Dad's face was staring out at me, the distance between him and Mum still great, Jacinta still had that fake smile plastered on her face, and I still looked as miserable as ever. Nothing had changed, really. Dad was dead, but that was the extent of it.

We were miserable in the photos, just as we were miserable now.

Keep tonight free, I messaged Colton, fingers flying over the surface of my tabloid. *I'm going to need your car.*

And my thumb presumably? Colton returned almost instantaneously, for the first time that day.

That's why you're invited.

Aren't you working tonight?

No, I definitely wasn't. I was fed up of everything. I refused to assign myself to an evening of being a commodity. I liked my job, but if this was the only occasion I was going to be allowed out of the house then I wasn't wasting it on waitressing.

Skipping mandatory work is illegal.

I know, Colt. Consider this a romantic gesture. Also, if I stay in the house any longer I'm going to murder someone.

A few seconds later the message *Murder is illegal too* came through.

Good to know my boyfriend had such a sound knowledge of the law. I rolled my eyes and pulled my TTC back into my central tabloid, closing the conversation and taking a few deep breaths.

I could survive this. My mother could not possibly keep me locked up in this house for ever. Nor could the Education Centre continue pushing the farming career (although, of course, this either ended in being a farmer or not . . . but one way or the other, the daily meetings with Mary Cuttleworth would not be continuing for much longer). Mum would stop looking at me like I was the devil incarnate. Jacinta would forgive me. I would actually get to *see* Colton without skipping out on work.

'Corin,' Mum said, stepping into my bedroom with a cup of tea. She set it down on my desk with a clink before turning to face me, her face purposefully composed. 'I am not trying to make you miserable.'

'Well, you are,' I said, glancing at the cup of tea suspiciously. 'I'm not particularly meaning to upset you, either.'

'I will do whatever it takes to ensure your welfare.'

'Little creepy,' I said.

Mum nodded once. 'You'll thank me one day, Corin.'

I watched her walk out and close the door behind her, suddenly needing to open up one of those old conversations with a fellow cynic and talk about all this. This is what happened when people were ignorant: they grounded their nineteen-year-old daughters for no reason, passive aggressively forcing them into marrying some predetermined *name* when they were just kids. If my mum was a cynic, she wouldn't have forced this on me.

'I doubt it,' I said to the closed door, messaging Colton with details about where he should pick me up.

'Hey,' I said, tapping on Colton's car window and grinning, 'stop warming up the driver's seat and get out.'

'Not being chased by an angry mob?' Colton said, getting out of the car and pausing to kiss me hello.

'No,' I said, pulling away for a split second, 'but there's no guarantee my mother doesn't have someone following me, so let's save the slush for when we've successfully ditched the place.'

'Where are we going?'

'Personally,' I said, sitting down in the driver's seat and taking a deep breath, 'I'm hoping to drive off the end of England and wind up in a different section.'

It was beginning to get warmer now. I pressed the button to open the window on my side.

'Not sure that's how cars work,' Colton said, dutifully leaning over and pressing his thumb against the recognition pad, 'and I thought we'd decided against joint suicide?'

'Yeah, well, I'm flexible.'

'I'd rather you weren't that flexible,' Colton said, 'if it's all the same to you.'

'I can deal with it,' I said, feeling the accelerator underneath my foot for a few seconds before I set the car into motion. 'Good God, I swear if I have to spend another day in that Education Centre someone is going to pay.'

'Nice to see you too.'

I gritted my teeth. It was OK for Colton. His family was nice and supportive, and his whole world wasn't constricting and becoming progressively more crap as things went on.

I hadn't realized how much I'd been relying on some stupid political movement to keep me together; now that was gone too, just because my crazy sister couldn't keep her hands off my tabloid.

'Well,' I said, foot pressing down on the accelerator as we hit one of the old motorways, deserted and barely used these days, because cities were near enough self-contained units. Why would you ever need to leave? 'After this, I'm probably going to be arrested rather than grounded, so I suspect I won't be seeing you for a while.'

'They're hardly going to arrest you for skipping work.'

'I left my TTC back at home,' I said. 'Turn yours off.'

'That's—'

'Illegal, yes. However, if you don't my mum's going to send someone out to fetch us in about half an hour, and I'm going to need at least an hour to be able to breathe.'

'Are you OK?'

'No,' I said firmly, 'definitely not. Next stupid question?'

'We're not . . . legitimately driving off the end of the country here?'

'No,' I said. 'I'm not crazy, Colton. We'll be back home in a couple of hours.'

'OK,' Colton said. 'Fine. Although if you could drive a little slower, that would be wonderful.'

'That's only going to make us later,' I said. 'Turn off your TTC. Only for an hour. Don't worry about it – I used to do it all the time.'

'That hardly makes me feel better.' Colton grinned. 'What laws haven't you broken?'

'Mostly the violence ones,' I said through gritted teeth, 'although that's only a testament to my self-control. Sorry about this,' I added. 'Bit of a breakdown going on.'

'Noted. Where *are* we going?'

'My dad's crash site.'

'You're such a romantic,' Colton said, eyes fixing on the

side of my face. 'First the place you broke up with your old boyfriend, now the place your dad died.'

'Jacinta went there on the anniversary, she said his memorial plaque had been ripped up . . . But she was being crazy. I want to . . . I want to see whether or not it's true.'

'Fair enough,' Colton said.

'Sorry I've been needy with the messaging,' I said, eyes set ahead on the road, 'and that I'm being moody and irritable. Things aren't good at the moment.'

'You don't have to apologize,' Colton said, 'and aren't you always moody and irritable?'

'Yes,' I said, 'but usually it's intended to be vaguely good-natured. Right now, I just feel vicious.'

'Just relax,' Colton said. 'Just . . . Corin, forget about everything for an hour or two . . . otherwise, there's really no point in this grand escape plan.'

'Exactly,' I said, taking a deep breath as I turned down the last road and pulled over. 'I think it's here.'

'Is this a good idea, Corin?'

'It's the best idea I've had in months,' I said, leaning over to kiss him for a few moments.

Now this, I'd missed. It was easy to get lost in a moment and feel a little *good* about yourself when someone was kissing you. And it was easy to forget about my family and the fact that my life was going nowhere when someone's lips were pressed against mine.

'Are you OK?'

'Well,' I said, pressing my forehead against his, 'not really.

Everyone's life seems to be moving forward and I'm just *stuck* here, Colton, and it's really crap.'

'So you're jealous?'

'Yes, I'm jealous,' I said, wrapping my fingers around Colton's jacket and not letting him go. 'I'm the nineteen-year-old, grounded, stuck with a stupid family in a stupid job living out this near *purgatory* where apparently I don't even have a choice about who I want to date.'

'That choice is me, right?'

'Yeah,' I said, kissing him again, 'definitely you. Now, I want to check out this memorial plaque.'

I undid my seat belt, stepping out onto the side of the road.

My dad had died here.

It didn't seem like a particularly remarkable place. I thought I'd be able to see the blood, feel the destruction, or at least be able to imagine how the car had swerved off the road, but I couldn't. Maybe the road layout had changed, but the picture of my dad bleeding and dying just didn't fit with this piece of road.

I bent down next to the place where, theoretically, his car had swerved and hit before it caught fire.

Jacinta was right, though. The memorial wasn't there. The screws had been picked out by some crude hand-made tool, the outline of the metal still there. There was just a trace of something that had been there once, exactly like my father.

'Corin, you OK?' Colton asked, still sitting in the passenger seat.

'Brilliant,' I said, heading back towards the car with a grimace.

Colton was a little too warm, but I liked it: it was comforting when it wasn't too much. I quite liked to overload all of my senses in any way possible. Not in the way that Jacinta blocked things out, by numbing her senses with pills from the hospital, but my way – becoming well and truly distracted by another person.

'Hey—'

'If you ask me if I'm OK one more time, Colt, I swear I'm going to hurt you.'

'All right,' Colton said, grinning for a second. 'I just haven't seen you so stressed since your dad's anniversary.'

'Jacinta . . .'

'I should have known it was something to do with Jacinta.'

'She just saw something on my computer,' I said, face twisting into a grimace at the memory. Colton raised his eyebrows at me suggestively. 'Shut up,' I said, half laughing. 'No . . . it was about my contact.'

'Ah.'

'Why has she always got to interfere?'

'Don't ask me,' Colton said. 'My sister can't talk yet. Well, she can't manage my name or sentences. It would be pretty hard for her to rat on me about anything.'

'Lucky,' I said, relaxing into Colton's arm and shutting my eyes for a second. 'I had to delete everything.'

'That's crap,' Colton said, finger brushing my fringe back

from my face for a second. 'You . . . you can use my tabloid if you like.'

'What?' I asked, shifting round in my seat to stare at him. Colton looked especially good today, although I'd chalked that up to not seeing him for ages, or maybe it was just the words he'd just said. Out loud. To me.

'To access your stuff,' Colton said. 'Obviously it's important to you.'

I reached up and kissed Colton properly, shifting over to his side of the car, hands balled up in the material of his jacket. 'I think I could marry you,' I said, staring at him. 'Are you serious?'

'On this occasion.'

Obviously I couldn't start the hard-core cynicism stuff on Colton's tabloid without explaining the whole situation to him (which was something I was most definitely not planning on doing at the moment – I was still going with subtly easing him into the issue), but I could send a few messages to Ean and get a few more books . . . re-download the footage for the D'livere (which I needed) and not have lost *everything* I'd managed to collect. Besides, I didn't know how long I could survive without having a different world to escape into.

'Thank you,' I said, pressing my lips against his.

Colton parked a street away from my house in order for us to say goodbye, although I didn't much fancy it at the moment.

I wasn't even sure how Colton had become so important, but apparently my sense of hating all people didn't quite stretch to him any more. He was the best of a bad lot, at any rate, and tolerating him really didn't seem that difficult. Instead, I was continually bemused at how much he seemed to tolerate from me; Colton might have the appearance of a guy unconcerned by getting into trouble or the like, but I was sure he'd never broken the law before. Even the stupid ones that everyone broke.

I was a terrible influence.

'Sometimes,' I said, head resting under Colton's chin, 'I wonder whether the inventor of the car knew they'd be used to make out in for centuries.'

'He had all the Romeo and Juliets in mind.'

'Tragic lovers like us,' I said, rolling my eyes. 'Wherefore art thou Colton Furnish?'

'In the passenger seat, where you relegated me to,' he answered, deliberately misunderstanding, although Shakespeare's actual meaning, I realized, *was* very apt.

'Sorry,' I grinned into the skin of his neck.

'One day I'm going to be allowed to drive my car again.'

I kissed the spot under his ear before pulling back and looking up at him. 'I really wouldn't count on it.'

'Well, any time you want to drive to a probably inappropriate place and then make out is fine by me.'

'Seriously,' I said, closing my eyes tightly, 'believe me when I say I'm not one to talk about my feelings, or usual lack of feelings, or act myself around pretty much anyone . . . but you're a nice guy, Colt, and I'm really quite glad that I've met you. But please remember that referencing *Romeo and Juliet* in public indicates you've read the play and is likely to drop me in a lot of trouble.'

'Corin,' Colton said, the moment stagnant for a second, a brief spot of calm, and then he was shifting back the side-arm of the passenger seat.

I wish I could have frozen the moment there, got out of the car and walked the few metres back to my house (as we were literally only parked so as not to be directly in front of it), but Colton had other ideas.

He was saying something — something about me that would probably have made me want to vomit if I'd listened — but I was too damn distracted because he was reaching for the catch on his wrist guard. He'd twisted it, a thrill of dread sparking up in my chest, and then — he was still talking but my brain couldn't process both his movement and his words at the same time — and then his wrist guard was off and his wrist was exposed.

And the name on Colton's wrist was *Corin*.

15

The Wrong Corin

There were a few moments of clarity before the whole scene became slightly wobbly.

Colton was sitting in the passenger seat, without a wrist guard, and the name *Corin* was written across his skin.

I slipped into a state of shock. I didn't know what to do. I took in a breath of air.

Silence.

There was a knock on the window on my side of the car. There was a police officer outside. I got out of the car. I was still feeling slightly shocked.

The man reached out, grabbed the bare skin of my arm and, after that, nothing made much sense: the chronology of everything was distorted and wrong. I was jumping from being in the car and staring at my name, to being out of the car and staring at the police officer.

I tumbled out onto the street. I could feel my mouth moving, but I had no idea what I was saying. Nothing made any sense.

Back in Colton's car, I was watching him taking off his wrist guard.

I felt seasick, even though I'd never experienced the sensation before; my brain was swimming, unable to focus on anything, but dragging through moments a little too slowly and sending my vision into snapshots that didn't quite fit together.

I remembered seeing the raised, red flesh of my name written across Colton's skin. I knew that it was my name. I recognized that much, but every thought as to why my name *might* be scrawled there had evaporated away. Because it didn't make sense . . . none of this made sense . . .

Everything was too vivid. Reality seemed to have slipped into one of those lucid effervescent dreams: a heavy hallucination that was too intense to be real and too real to be a figment of the imagination. Mouth dry. Eyes blinking but still seeing. Limbs slack.

My name, there, across the blue of his veins and the caramel flesh: *Corin*.

Me, except not me.

The knock on the window barely seemed like reality, but Colton was hurriedly trying to refasten his wrist guard — blocking my name from sight — and I'd tumbled out of the car to where I was standing now, shocked and confused.

Jarring, jolty scenes.

The man was there, the one who'd knocked on the window and saved me from the moment: dark skin and dark expression.

He was wearing a police uniform.

Everything was icy cold except the heat that seemed to stem from the place where the man had touched my arm, spreading outwards over my body and pushing away the searing burn of the cold.

Drugged, then.

That made sense. Or, at least, as much sense as anything made in a world where my skin was written across Colton's wrist, and a police officer was pressing some drugged patch onto my arm, and the world was twisting into a confusion of the past and the present and, *What was going on?*

'— Corin Blacksmith.'

The knock on the window. A man. I remembered his dark hands closing around my wrist and the *click* of the handcuffs that encased them. *Oh.* I'd been handcuffed.

'I'm afraid you have to come with me—'

— Colton exiting the car, the car door slamming, words exchanged —

— then there was the knowledge that Colton's carpinomen is me, but not me —

— and the man was there, and I was in handcuffs, barely thinking to object and —

— the growing, burning, all-encompassing heat from my arm —

'What the *hell* is going on?'

My brain was still stuck in limbo, my body moving

automatically as the man tried to get me to move forward. *One step. Another step. Focus on motion. Forward.*

'I think I'm being arrested,' I said, summoning up sarcasm from somewhere and straining slightly against the handcuffs, 'although I think I'm due my rights being read out.'

'Move out of my way, sir—'

'You've got the wrong Corin,' Colton said, grabbing hold of the man's arm. 'You can't just—'

The wrong Corin.

Yes, that was me. I was the wrong Corin. Colton was searching for a girl named Corin who was not me. He must have thought it was me, but it was not me. I was wrong. I was all wrong. I was the wrong person. I was not what he was looking for. I was . . . I was wrong.

I was . . .

. . . being led towards the police car parked outside my house.

'You've *drugged her*,' Colton yelled, pushing forward. 'That's not . . . *You've got this all wrong.*'

'What's happening?'

Jacinta. My sister. Not robotic or dead, or even the monster I'd become used to, but reinstated as the sister that I used to know. I wanted to reach out. I wanted to reach out and *grab* her, but she was firing questions at the police officer, her fingers scrabbling against my flesh as she tried to pull me away.

'On what charges?' she was saying.

'I don't know,' I said, voice slurring, unsure whether the question was directed at me or not. 'Jacinta, I don't know.'

I got a glimpse of my sister. She was wearing her pyjamas, expression livid, animated, alive. Her hands closed around my arm, the same arm that was burning with heat and sensation and—

Clarity seemed to settle around my brain slightly, enough that I was able to assume Jacinta had done something to stop the patch on my arm twisting my brain function. I looked down at it. She'd ripped off the patch, leaving a slightly red area of skin.

I glanced up at my house, and it was then that I saw my mother at the window . . . expression fixed into a hard line before she drew the curtains together and blocked herself from my sight.

It reminded me of all those moments I thought I'd seen my dead father.

Again, it was just a hallucination because if my mother had been at the window, any second now she'd be flying out onto the street and objecting to what was happening . . . what was happening. What *was* happening?

Then I was bundled into the back of the car, another burst of heat was pressed against my arm, and the motion of the car rocked me straight into the oblivion of unconsciousness.

The jarred nature of time continued after I lost consciousness. I was remembering things, floating through memories and moments, twisting and thinking and realizing.

I was the wrong Corin.

*　*　*

I could see an image of Colton, years ago, all caramel colouring and self-satisfied smile even then. And we were back in a pre-level class delivering our bonding stories. I was standing up at the front, stonily retelling my parents' tale without emotion (they'd been arguing again, if I remember rightly). And Colton was watching me.

Colton always did seem a little too interested in me, back when we were younger . . . I'd chalked it up to me having a bit of a reputation thanks to my exploits with various Thomases and Jacinta, and my father (losing a parent wasn't exactly common), but now that I really thought about it, it pre-dated that by quite a while. I supposed that Colton had always thought me interesting, always entertained the possibility that I might be the one for him, knowing that my name matched the one on his wrist.

And he hadn't been concerned that I'd never paid any attention to him because there were so many Coltons in the Education Centre that I'd have limitless options to sift through.

Of course.

Colton driving his pretty car, fingers nervously tapping over the dashboard, him delivering me a killer line in resigning me to shock.

'It's just, Corin, there is a slight difference between Tom and Thomas. And T-O-M-A-S Tomas too, for that matter. So, as a girl with more than a couple of brain cells, you'd know that. So if you genuinely thought T-O-M-A-S Tomas, or T-H-O-M-A-S

Thomas, was your soul mate then you'd have known that T-O-M Tom was not.'

'This isn't a spelling test.'

'Either way, you'd have known that the name on Tom's wrist was not going to be Corin. So you framed him to make him look like a heartless bastard.'

'Are you going somewhere with this?'

'So I'd hazard a tentative guess that your carpinomen isn't a variation of Thomas at all. You picked that name and decided to convince everyone it was your carpinomen while working your way through all the Toms and Thomases the Education Centre has to offer.'

I'd never asked why he was interested enough to think about my carpinomen. I'd never thought to question it. I'd never thought to ask him *why* it had mattered to him enough to dig through all my lies and question my sodding spelling abilities.

I'd never asked. I hadn't even been interested until he'd revealed he was a puer immanis.

The car again.

'Do you have a carpinomen?'

'Why don't you check and see?'

My fear, in that moment, had been all tied up in the idea of a *blank wrist* and the fact that Colton thought that I, as a girl who ignored her carpinomen, could be a way to make sure he didn't wind up alone.

* * *

'*That's a ridiculous rumour. Of course I have a carpinomen. It's a great one too.*'

'*I bet mine's better. Mine's brilliant.*'

'*Of course it is. I could hardly imagine the other piece of your soul being anything other than spectacular.*'

Colton had thought I'd known my name was on his wrist. All the time I thought we'd both been on the same page, it seemed Colton had been reading a completely different novel – his was some bonding story that we'd tell our children, while mine had been some act of rebellion *and* . . .

'*But let's just say you'd met your carpinomen and you wanted to start a relationship with him . . . no one's going to believe you're anima-vinculum because you've spent four years creating a rather convincing story that it's Thomas.*'

'*You didn't believe it.*'

'*Yeah.*'

'Well,' I said, '*why wouldn't everyone else notice?*'

Let's just say . . . he'd practically told me and I'd been too self-absorbed to even notice the issue. Hell, I'd always been self-absorbed when it came to Colton.

Colton liked to trace shapes on the back of my wrist, just above my wrist guard.

I hadn't understood why . . . but now it was obvious. He was just reminding himself that we were meant to be together.

Me in my room and Colton in his, communicating through our tabloids, talking about wrist font.
 Colton had typed out my name and messaged it to me.

He'd been checking the wrist font against his own wrist. He'd been making sure it was accurate. Wasn't that near enough the first thing I'd done? Typed out my carpinomen before obliterating it (because I hated my carpinomen to the extreme)?

I'd typed Colton *back.*

This wasn't his fault. I wanted this to be his fault. I wanted to blame him for making assumptions but there wasn't enough to pin on him.
 Only, this ruined everything I thought I liked about Colton. I liked him because he liked me despite all the numerous reasons why he shouldn't – because he took my sarcasm and bitterness in his stride, dug a little deeper and was determined to find out *why* I was the way I was. And all that had been because he thought that we were soul mates the whole damn time, filling up another page of our bonding story with each conversation, writing whole chapters about the ways that he could fix me.
 Which isn't what I wanted.
 He hadn't been understanding or accepting. He hadn't been some figure of *hope*, showing that I wasn't so bad,

actually, and that humanity wasn't so bad. He'd had a purpose in all of this. He hadn't cared about *me* at all.

This was all just some stupid story and I hadn't even realized.

Sure he probably had some feelings towards me, but not the sort that I thought they'd been . . . No, his had been the sort that rose out of a sense of obligation, the sort of feeling that came from seeing a person *every day* and wondering whether they were the one you'd spend the rest of your life with.

Only, he'd got it wrong.

Which meant that Jacinta was right to warn me. I was in the definite wrong for letting this relationship happen, and the whole thing was seconds away from crashing to absolute ruin . . . I'd have to explain to Colton that this was all a big fat misunderstanding, explain the whole cynicism movement and hope he liked me enough to say *balls* to the other Corin.

Except he wouldn't. I knew he wouldn't.

So it was probably a god-awful time to realize how much I cared about him.

When I woke, my wrist guard had been removed.

I felt nauseous and slightly enthralled as I traced a finger across the name that was written there.

Z. My head still didn't feel clear from the drugs.

A. I was in what looked to be some hidden corner of the hospital.

I. The ward was large but empty, as though it had just been deserted and all the beds carried away.

D. Obviously the place had been designed to make me feel uncomfortable.

E. I'd been dressed in one of the standard hospital gowns I'd seen Jacinta wear so often.

N. A man emerged, dressed in a suit and one of those superior expressions.

He glanced down at my exposed wrist, taking in the word written there.

'Come with me,' he said, uninterested.

Zaiden.

16
Autonomy

The man was paler than should be possible, clearly the result of some hyper white-inbreeding and a dislike of the outside world. In fact, he looked like someone had edited his appearance and switched him over to greyscale – colourless grey hair (although he seemed a little too young for it), grey eyes, a pallid complexion and lips that barely seemed separate from the rest of his face.

'Sit down, Corin Blacksmith,' he said, expression twisting up into a smile. 'I would like to talk to you.'

'Seems like a convoluted method,' I said, heart thudding erratically in my chest. 'Arrest and drugging.'

'Effective, you'll agree?' he asked. 'I am Henrik Walcott.'

His name stuck in my brain. He'd been on the electoral

roll, amongst a bunch of equally unappetizing candidates, for one of the positions on the council.

Politics always made me angry. They made a big deal out of the main elections, even though the power our President had was so minimal he was basically inconsequential – voted for only as a pretty face to sit in on worldwide meetings. His instructions were drip-fed from those who pulled the strings. He was a chess piece. Entirely separate from the brain behind the game. And besides, I'd voted for the blonde bombshell with the killer legs – if we were to have a pointless face to represent us, I'd rather it be Grace Shellcot than Henrik Walcott, or Matthu Simmons, the middle-aged prat who'd actually won.

'I voted against you in the last councillor elections,' I said, feeling my legs shaking slightly. I walked forward and sat down in the vacant seat, reminding myself that there was nothing more intimidating about his side of the desk than mine, and any imbalance of power was an entirely fictitious state of mind.

Henrik Walcott could not *possibly* have a significant amount of power. He was simply like Mary Cuttleworth, a man instructed to act by the higher-ups. It was just a lack of awareness as to who the higher-ups were that made me feel slightly uncomfortable.

His gaze drifted towards my wrist. He was not repulsed by the exposed flesh or the name written there. He drank in the power of the situation. He must know thousands of carpinomens. He must have known the truth about so many people's souls that he no longer remembered them all. It must be strange to be so desensitized to something so conditioned to repulse.

'Thankfully the population at large has better sense than you, Ms Blacksmith.'

'I reserve judgement on that,' I said, stretching out my fingers. 'Is this about my vote, then? Seems like an interesting political campaign.'

'I am sure you are aware that would be illegal.' Henrik Walcott smiled. 'I am here to discuss the cynicism movement.'

My brain stuck on the words, processing, trying to work out what he was saying. 'The cynicism movement?' I questioned, glancing towards the door.

'You're an intelligent girl, Ms Blacksmith,' Henrik said, smiling. 'Let's not play dumb with me.'

'OK,' I said, 'fine. I know it's a sham. You put the names on people's wrists.'

'Indeed,' Henrik said. 'In actual fact, I picked out *your* carpinomen sixteen years ago. It seems you were not happy with my choice?'

I'd never had this confirmed to me before. I'd pretty much convinced myself of its truth: everything I'd found and been sent pointed towards this conclusion, but it was another thing having the suspicions I barely felt comfortable thinking about in public proved correct.

Everyone's whole future was determined by some individual with a serious power complex. All this talk of souls and soul mates, and it was merely a man-made phenomenon that we were conditioned to believe. Another thing determined by a government I hadn't voted for.

'It shouldn't *be* your choice,' I said, closing my hand around my wrist so that I didn't have to look at it. It was a repulsive stretch of skin. I hated the way you could see the blue hue of your veins, the line where your hand started, how truly easy it was to hurt yourself. One slit and you were bleeding out.

I'd seen how much wrists could bleed.

'You are more acquainted with history than the average teenager,' Henrik said, his expression still serene, 'and yet there are still great holes within your knowledge.'

'I *know* that it didn't use to be like this,' I said, my grip tightening around my wrist.

'Indeed,' Henrik said, 'the world was entirely different.'

'They actually gave a damn about people's rights.'

Henrik smiled as though my comment had been expected. The expression flared up the deep-set incredulity I'd been hoarding in my chest ever since I'd first *doubted*. I'd never intended to become a cynic. I hadn't known what I was searching for. I just knew that I needed more.

This man dictated people's lives and he didn't even care if it all went wrong.

'The reports from the Education Centre have always shown that you are inquisitive. But you disappoint me, Corin.'

'Greatly sorry,' I spat, straightening up in my seat.

'You've failed to ask the most important question.'

'Where's the ladies' room?'

'*Why?*'

The silence settled over us. I'd barely looked at the room,

being too transfixed by the entirely colourless Henrik, but now I wanted to do anything but look at him: the walls were white too, the floor laminate, the desk ancient and wooden. The place looked more like something out of one of those old films than from my reality.

I wanted to know.

I'd longed to be given an explanation as to *why* I was expected to benignly walk through my life without thinking or making any real choices.

I'd dreamed constantly about having someone *finally* tell me something that made the world make sense.

I wanted to know why I was to be assigned a career and a house and a life partner more than I'd ever wanted anything. The need for an explanation had near driven me mad.

I was stuck in a limbo of being desperate for answers, not wanting to satisfy the odious man in front of me by asking the question, and a sudden edgy fear that I wasn't ready to know.

'You have not asked me, Corin, why we print names on our children's wrists.'

'Why?' I asked, rolling my eyes. 'Do tell me. I would love to be let into your little *inner* circle.'

Sarcasm was my usual mask to hide my feelings, but Henrik's smile made me feel he knew that my heart was thudding erratically; my brain was icily clear and it was very difficult to breathe.

This was it.

'People are not capable of making their own decisions,' Henrik said simply. 'They choose badly. They pick careers on a whim, they sleep around, they break laws, they hurt people, they break other people's hearts.' His grey eyes seemed to sharpen slightly as he stared at me, as if trying to make a point that I had done *all* of those things and more. I was hardly an advertisement for making correct decisions. This was personal. This was an accusation.

Apparently it was my fault the whole world was no longer allowed choices. What a bloody joke.

'Humanity had an irresponsible number of children, an irresponsible number of sexual partners, they took drugs and got drunk, neglected to take care of the earth, spread across every surface of the planet with houses and no thought to the consequences of the destruction of farming land. The earth's resources were finite, running out. People were going to die, Ms Blacksmith, and they were going to suffer. And what did humanity say? They said, *If it's not me then I am not interested.*'

'Sounds like humanity,' I said, crossing my arms over my chest as though the extra pressure of arm against the outside of my ribcage might cause my heart to slow down slightly. *Thump. Thump. Thump.* No such luck.

'We destroyed forests and beaches and countryside. We made mountains of our rubbish. We pursued human knowledge rather than happiness. Women were raped as strategies in wars. We threatened each other with nuclear weapons that would have killed thousands. We tried to cure the diseases affecting the rich and ignored the rest. We damn near destroyed the planet in our pursuit of *goods*. We slaughtered each other in the name of God. Children did not know who their fathers were. Children's needs weren't considered. Some were not given access to education; others were crippled by a flawed education system. People were unhappy, but they believed the only route to happiness was to *gain* more money, possessions, status symbols. Do you understand, Ms Blacksmith? We were running the world into the ground. We were destroying ourselves.'

'Yeah,' I said, 'nice speech. What happened to good old-fashioned freedom?'

Henrik was entirely still throughout his speech. 'Several hundred years ago, when the world was on the brink of ruin, the decision was made. It was not, as you would have it, forced upon humanity, but chosen. When asked, would you like to continue on the road to wanton destruction or would you like all moral responsibility to be taken away from you? The people chose *the reformation.*'

'So a bunch of men sat in a room and planned out a whole pretty society,' I said, my mouth dry. 'Because a couple of people made a few stupid mistakes?'

'Billions of people,' Henrik said. 'Billions of people like you, Corin. Flawed people who think *nothing* of the consequences their actions have on others.'

'But . . . soul mates?'

'Yes,' Henrik agreed. 'A rather clumsy aspect of the plan, I'll admit. I voted for it to be overturned, you understand, but it is too late for that. Too many people *believe in it.*'

'And that's OK, is it?'

'People are happy,' Henrik said, 'and we come to an arrangement with those who aren't.'

'An arrangement?'

'Ms Blacksmith,' Henrik drawled, looking even more amused, 'you do not believe that you're the first person to discover the truth? Surely your inflated sense of worth isn't that great? Hundreds of people are aware of the truth. Far more than your little cynicism project would allow. Who do you think runs the country? Who do you think picks out pairs? Who filters out the media? Who prints the names on the skin? Who watches to make sure people are not about to find out *en masse*?'

'And I suppose now you think I'll help?'

'No,' Henrik said. 'I neither want nor need your help, Ms Blacksmith. I have much higher calibre people to choose from.'

'Lovely. I guess that means you're not voting for me, either?'

'You are inconsequential,' Henrik said, waving this away. 'From the look of the files on your TTC, you have done nothing more than take an interest. Do you realize, Corin, that every year there are hundreds of teenagers who plan revolts and start recruiting? There are those prepared to kill themselves to persuade others to take notice. And what, Ms Blacksmith, did you do with this information you found?'

Nothing is what I'd done. I'd sat on it. I'd reached out and found a few other people who didn't believe, like I did, became bitter and angry. I'd dated a series of guys called Thomas and made a name for myself as a slut.

I hadn't told Jacinta, who'd tried to kill herself on the basis of a lie.

I hadn't told Josaphine, whose parents had stuck together

despite the fact that their sexualities hadn't matched up.

I'd started to tell Colton, but obviously he hadn't noticed anything at all because he was too blissful at the thought that the two of us were anima-vinculum.

'Did you time this with Colton's big reveal, or what?'

'Yes,' Henrik said, smiling slightly. 'We tried to push you away from him, Ms Blacksmith. Are you sure you want freedom of choice, Corin Blacksmith?'

'Quite sure,' I said, 'but I want to know more.'

'Understandable,' Henrik said. 'What would you like to know?'

'So, what, years ago everyone just *agreed* to this and you started printing names on people's wrists? Weren't they bothered?'

'The first generation of parents signed the consent for the children,' Henrik said, 'and thus, a lie began. Just like Father Christmas, and all those other fairy tales.'

'Except you kept it up,' I said, 'for their whole lives. So they then told *their* children, without questioning it?'

'Plenty of questions,' Henrik said, 'but the fact is, Corin, people are happy. No one ends up alone. A large part of a successful relationship is a willingness for it to work out, so most couples stay together and raise their families. There is little to no variation in the size of families, which means wealth is more evenly distributed and each family has all the room they need.'

'A willingness for it to work out?' I demanded. 'Are *you* married?'

'Yes,' Henrik said, holding up a hand. I glanced at his

silver wedding band, trying to picture him at home with two kids and a wife. I couldn't. He was too grey. He was too much a part of this office and a part of politics to exist outside this context.

'And is she your carpinomen?'

'She is now,' Henrik said, lips twisting up into a smile, 'although I admit hers was not my original name.'

'What the hell are you talking about?' I demanded.

Henrik smiled. I decided that I hated him. I hated everything from his prematurely grey hair (and possibly surgery-enhanced face) to the suit he'd picked out to try and intimidate me. I hated the way his gaze drifted over to my wrist as though it didn't matter. I hated the idea that he'd been the one to pick out the name for me, doing God knows what to make sure it stuck there for years on end . . . I hated the fact that he didn't seem to *care* that he was tearing my whole world apart with a few choice words.

'As I said,' Henrik said, leaning forward, 'we come to an arrangement with those who are not happy.'

'What?'

'We are not unreasonable,' Henrik said. 'We understand couples picked out when you were very young do not always work out. We permit changes to be made under certain circumstances.'

'What circumstances?'

'We keep an eye on things.'

'So you've been spying on us?' I demanded. 'That's how you know about this, right? Because you've been spying on everyone.'

'Don't be ridiculous,' Henrik said, smiling. 'And you wonder why we've banned most sensationalist literature? It is hardly necessary for us to spy, when other people are so willing to do so. A source tipped us off and informed us we should take a look at your hard drive.'

Jacinta.

Jacinta had sold me out to these *people* because she'd read a bunch of stupid things on my computer. She'd had the audacity to pretend to be shocked when I was arrested, running out onto the street as if any of it was a surprise. I swallowed.

'You'll be upset to note that your good friend Ean Broth has been removed from his position in the Media Network.'

'Not really,' I muttered.

'He's been incarcerated for sexual offences with an underage girl.'

'I don't remember any offences,' I said, folding my arms and glaring at the man.

'The law includes conversation,' Henrik said, 'and I must inform you, some of our best employees were shocked at the content of your inbox, Ms Blacksmith.'

'Well,' I said, 'I wanted to know what was going on.'

'Clearly,' Henrik said, his lips once again twisting into a smile. 'Did you have any more questions, Ms Blacksmith?'

'Why are you answering my questions?'

'It seems you previously objected to being lied to,' Henrik said, shrugging his shoulders as he pulled out an actual *paper file* with my name written on it. 'We know a great deal about you, Corin Blacksmith, and we would prefer that you were content.'

'Content? You want me to be content?'

'Isn't that what any government wants for its people?'

'No,' I said, 'it's not.'

'You're far too cynical,' Henrik said, grinning at his own joke, before opening the file and pulling out a few pieces of paper. 'You do not wish to know how we chose carpinomen? When we are prepared to waive them? How we ensure everyone has a partner?'

'Yes,' I said, too distracted to come up with something sarcastic and scathing. 'I do want to know that.'

'I am inviting you to ask.'

'Well, sorry,' I said heatedly. 'I've got a lot on my mind right now.'

The Colton issue was pressing in the back of my mind. I hadn't even realized how much the rejection of being the wrong Corin hurt until I thought about his name; it wasn't like I was head over heels in love with the guy, but he'd accepted me . . . apparently that acceptance had only stretched so far because I was his carpinomen. Apparently the whole time I'd been struck by him being a nice, attractive guy who had a few things in common with me, he'd been thinking about the story we'd tell our children.

'The domestic with your boyfriend?' Henrik asked. 'Like I said, we tried to push you away . . . but you are very stubborn, Corin. If I had been directly involved in the decision, I would have stopped pushing the two of you apart . . . it was much more likely to crumble without our interference. Still, that's quite a mess you've got yourself into.'

'Why do you care?' I demanded. 'It doesn't matter what

you say, Walcott, I'm still not going to start voting for you.'

'Good,' Henrik said. 'I rather don't want your vote, Ms Blacksmith.'

'And why's that?'

'Because I think you make very bad decisions.'

'I haven't had much chance to make decisions,' I said, glaring up at him. 'Thanks to someone, my autonomy has been severely restricted.'

'And yet,' Henrik said, 'you still appear to have broken at least two boys' hearts, dated two more, skipped work, broken the law and begun to self-destruct.'

'Yeah, well,' I said, 'I'm sure you're not perfect either.'

'Quite.'

'So, how *do* you pick everyone's carpinomen? Just a big database?'

'It's much more complicated than that,' Henrik said. 'There are children being born, all the time, and usually not with a perfect balance of male and female. Children, regrettably, also die. The database required is enormous, as you can imagine – every single birth is registered, added on, then put in the queue. We prefer to make matches within the same countries, although it is not always possible. We try and wait till the child is required to visit a hospital – broken leg, sprained ankle, injections etc. . . . although, of course, that's not always possible either. You were brought in for a routine check-up when you were three years old. You received your name after your match received yours. He had your name placed on his wrist nearly two years previously. Although, of course, you have not met him yet.'

'I don't want to.'

'So I have seen from the content of your tabloid. Were there any other questions?'

'The arrangements you come to,' I said. 'What do you mean?'

'Sometimes people fall in love, sometimes people die . . . it cannot be helped. Any more questions?'

'Yes, actually,' I said fiercely. 'What are you planning on doing to me?'

'Once again,' Henrik said, his grey eyes glinting in the dim light of his office, 'you have been reading too many story books. You are not in danger, Ms Blacksmith. You are not about to be incarcerated. We are merely meeting in order for me to make sure you have all the facts.'

'You've never bothered before.'

'Your diligence towards the pursuit of knowledge is one of your few admirable qualities.'

'I haven't worked out what any of yours are,' I spat back, 'but thanks for the compliment. So you're just going to let me walk right out of here when we're done?'

'No,' Henrik said. 'We're going to come to some arrangement.'

'OK,' I said, taking a deep breath, 'if you're going to keep bringing up these sodding *arrangements* then you're going to have to explain what you mean.'

'I intend to,' Henrik said. 'As I mentioned previously, we often come across those who stumble across the truth. It was a clumsy idea, originally, and I firmly believe that we should have stopped at streaming careers and assigning houses—'

'How liberal of you.'

'Actually, much more liberal than the person you voted for over me,' Henrik said, inclining his head towards me, 'but I do not have the power to overhaul the system. No one does. It is set in motion. It is *undoable*, Ms Blacksmith, and it is for the greater good. However, there are those who find out. There are several objections towards the system – sometimes, the individual is in love with someone else, or they are gay, or they simply object to the loss of their freedom.'

'Crazy.'

'Please save your sarcasm, Ms Blacksmith, I do not appreciate it.'

'I don't appreciate *this*.'

'We offer those people a choice,' Henrik said. 'We offer them a chance to prove that they are able to make their own decisions and live with the consequences of those decisions.'

'Generous.'

'Exactly,' Henrik said, 'and here are your choices.' He placed his hands over three pieces of paper he'd pulled out of my file, laying out each of them across the desk with another of his frustrating smiles. 'The first,' Henrik said, fingers skimming over the surface of the first document, 'is the choice to forget. We have the science available to block this out of your memory. You will go on living, happy in the knowledge that you have a soul mate out there and you are *meant* to be with another individual.'

'No thanks.'

'The second,' Henrik continued, glancing at me for a second, 'is to do nothing. Walk out of here, promise you will not reveal the truth to any others and live your life as you please. We will not make you marry anyone you do not wish to. You can either be alone, find your soul mate, or find another who doesn't care if you are not their carpinomen. But you will not tell *anyone* what you know.'

'What if I do?'

'I know four individual ways to make your life more uncomfortable, Ms Blacksmith, and that is without racking my brains to come up with any more. I am quite creative and it's in my interests to keep you quiet. In fact, all three options have that in common — you will remain silent.'

'What's number three?'

'Number three,' Henrik said, middle finger glossing over the sheets, 'is that we will make your carpinomen match your boyfriend's.'

I stared at him, gobsmacked.

'You will not have to explain to him that you are not his carpinomen, nor will you have to face up to the fact that you are not what he wants. It may trap you into a future with him, but perhaps that is preferable to the prospect of being alone . . . or indeed, with another individual whom you have never met? I do not know, Ms Blacksmith. I know what I think you should do, but this is your choice. This is your opportunity to carve out your own future.'

'What's with the papers?' I asked, my voice catching in my throat.

'Contracts. We rarely use paper, as you well know, but in this case it is important for filing reasons. Each contract is legally binding. You will read each one, make your decision and then live with the consequences. Any more questions?'

'Yes,' I said. 'What do you think I should do?'

'Option Two. Nothing,' Henrik said, standing up. 'You have as long as you want. Hopefully we will never see each other again. I hope you do not make a mistake, for your sake.'

He was much taller than I'd realized, stretching up to the ceiling like some oddly grey giant.

'Can I have my wrist guard back?' I asked.

'When you have made your decision,' Henrik said, nodding to me once more before he left the room.

The soft clunk of the door kick-started my emotional reaction to the whole thing.

Instantly I had a headache. I wasn't sure whether it was the aftermath of the drug they'd given me, or something else, but I wanted nothing more than to crawl back home and hibernate in bed.

It was true. The whole thing I'd believed in was *confirmed* and *true* and everyone was going through the motions because of some great big mistakes humanity made ages ago . . . and I wasn't sure whether the reasoning behind the thing made it better or worse. Even I could see the benefits of streaming everyone into careers and assigning houses . . . I could understand that humans made bad choices and shouldn't be *allowed* to burn up the earth with a series of projects they didn't think through . . . I could *understand* that.

I was hardly a supporter of humanity. I'd written off most people and had been let down by half the people I'd ever met. If I could have taken the ability to decide out of Jacinta's hands, then I would have done: if it had stopped her from taking the knife to her wrists, then I would have done anything.

I wasn't sure I could justify assigning someone a life partner. *Except* couples did stay together. *Except* families were uniform. If Jacinta hadn't deviated from the plan then . . . well, then this wouldn't have happened. Josaphine . . . her dad was gay and her mum was straight and they'd always seemed happy together. *Maybe* it was for the better. *Maybe*.

It didn't matter what I thought, that was clear, because I didn't have the power to change any of it. It was fact. All I had was three contracts and three options, a headache and no idea what I should do.

The name on my wrist was teasing me. Normally I didn't spend so much time looking at it. I hated the word printed there even though I'd never met anyone who had that name. I didn't want to know anything about this *Zaiden* who I was theoretically supposed to be with for ever. I didn't want anything to do with him. Every time I thought of the name I got angry, especially with the truth laid out there for all to see.

I pressed my knuckles into my forehead and pulled the contracts towards me. I had a *choice*. Despite myself, there was a thrill of pleasure at the idea of actually having *a choice*; of making my own decisions and my own mistakes, regardless of what anyone else thought or did.

Except this decision wasn't going to pollute the earth or damn thousands to hell. This choice could only do me damage, so it was the best of both worlds – choice with limits, choice with restrictions, choice without the fear of ruining everything. Only I didn't like any of the three choices.

None of them seemed right. None of them . . . none of them seemed to align with what I wanted.

I could barely read the print on the paper because my eyes wouldn't focus properly. I hadn't experienced paper before, not for years and certainly not like this. They'd given us some in intermediate pre-level classes, to try our hand at handwriting and drawing on paper. Not much, though. It was too unsustainable.

Forgetting seemed absurd. Forgetting was not an option I was prepared to even consider. I'd probably still get curious and search again, discovering the same thing and winding up back here. Besides, I didn't want them messing with my brain. I didn't care how good their surgeons were, I'd rather keep everyone's hands out of my brain.

I didn't know what to do.

The second option seemed OK. The third seemed convenient.

Maybe it would be better to forget?

I stared down at the name written across my wrist, lost in thought, before I forced myself to focus and began the business of reading each of the three contracts in detail.

17

Uncovering Jacinta

I felt like the house should be somehow different, because my whole perspective seemed to have shifted. The tint of the truth should have coloured everything differently, and the sameness of it all threw me. Everything was supposed to have changed.

There was nothing quite as disturbing as not being sure whether something was wrong or right, grappling with the morality and ethics and coming up with nothing but a grey area. I had been torn between hating humanity and hating all that we did, and still feeling that – intrinsically – I'd been due a chance to shape my own life and make my own decisions. *Except* none of my personal decisions had led to anything good. *Except* the government's actions in all of this had twisted my life horribly too. *And still* lurking behind these myriad thoughts was that other truth: it didn't matter what I thought about it, because that didn't make a damn difference to the reality of the situation. The world didn't ask *me* whether I was OK with something before it happened . . . I was stuck in this scenario with no emergency exit and no ejector seat (other than joining some of the other cynics and slicing off my carpinomen, which wasn't something I was prepared to do). My feelings towards it were worthless. My trains of thought were stagnant, dead ends that did nothing but tie me into knots.

The truth never set anyone free, of that I was sure.

I stepped through the front door, self-consciously twisting my wrist guard around my arm. Blinking, I stepped back into my tiny world — through the corridor, past the living room and into the kitchen.

Jacinta. The sting of her betrayal was fresh and I'd already decided that I simply wasn't going to talk to her. What was there to say? She'd sold me out.

'Corin,' Jacinta said, eyes sharpening as she looked at me. Her gaze travelled to the restlessness of my fingers, twisting and scrabbling at the band of metal that encircled my wrist. Her eyes narrowed, expression transforming into something that made me want to regress to someone younger and less responsible. Jacinta was not supposed to turn one of those expressions on me.

Irritation, yes, and perhaps disappointment and anger, but hatred was a little too much for me to handle from my sister's direction. Even though I was sure I was radiating the same expression in my gaze.

'So,' I said, shrugging my shoulders slightly, 'I guess I was arrested. Driving without insurance . . .' I continued, which was the lie printed across the release document they'd given me. I was still struggling to believe that I'd only been gone for twenty-four hours, because the world damn sure wasn't the same as it had been twenty-four hours ago. Worse, it had only been a month since fake Father's Day. How had so much happened? 'Although,' I said, tilting my head at my sister, 'you'd know all about that . . . given you handed me in to the authorities.'

I wondered if she felt bad about that. If she knew how huge the consequences had been for digging around on my computer . . . I hoped she felt bad about it. I wanted this to be one of the things that kept her awake in the middle of the night, because it was – without a doubt – the worst thing she'd ever done to me.

'How dare you,' Jacinta said, her voice so quiet I might not have heard her over my own breathing. 'How *dare* you.'

'I'm just saying,' I said, leaning against the kitchen counter. 'Mum's probably going to be pissed when she finds out that thanks to you, that I have a criminal record . . . actually, she'll probably congratulate you. Well done, Jacinta, you're doing a *grand job* of ruining my life.'

Jacinta's whole countenance had distorted. I didn't think I'd seen her so animated since the day, three weeks after she'd tried to forcefully remove her carpinomen, when she'd found out that Brett had moved away: I'd had actual nightmares about the mad expression in her eyes, her hands repeatedly tugging at her wrist guard as though she could make it disappear, and her body weight shifting from foot to foot in a perpetual state of agitated motion.

I shut up and took a step back away from her.

Jacinta closed the space by stepping forward, eyes flashing, and grabbing hold of my jacket. Her gaze bored into mine for a second, then flicked to the door, then back to me again. Her lips curved down into a frown. 'We're going out.'

'What?' I asked slowly. I'd been looking forward to the moment when I could collapse back in my bed and try not to think about all that had happened in the past twenty-four hours. I wanted to sleep before I had to start to process everything. I wanted to watch something trashy on my tabloid and ignore everything for a brief incubation period (especially my mum and my sister). I needed to map out how I was going to explain to Colton what had happened. Or not explain. The driving without insurance was a good-enough cover, but I wasn't quite ready to dive back into lying just yet. I needed a break. Screw a short nap, I needed a lengthy coma to file everything properly in my head.

Plus, Jacinta was bloody terrifying when she was like this.

'Come on,' she implored, tugging me forward. I tried to wriggle out of her grip, but somehow my gardener's muscles couldn't compete with Jacinta's sheer *will*. She had me back out the front door, throwing me towards the car and glaring at me in complete silence.

She got into the driver's seat and placed her thumb against the recognition pad.

I hated it when Jacinta drove anywhere. There were telltale signs that perhaps she wasn't as terrified of driving as she made out – the fact that sometimes the fuel was lower than when I'd left it, a dreamlike whiff of her perfume, the seat adjusted slightly to accommodate her extra height. I could count the number of times she'd wanted to drive with an audience on one hand, and certainly I had never seen her want to drive when she was in a state like this.

Jacinta's foot slammed onto the accelerator. She turned off the drive and onto the road at a speed even I wouldn't consider safe, her fingers white as she gripped the steering wheel. She wasn't blinking. Her whole body was straight as a rod, gaze fixed on the road, pushing at the accelerator as we gained speed.

Holy crap.

'Where the hell are we going?' I demanded, hands clutching the edge of the seat and my eyes wide. Jacinta had lost it. Finally, after all this build-up, she'd gone in-fucking-sane.

I couldn't imagine her looking any more mental. Even after she'd bloodied up her wrists, there'd been some sense of *peace* surrounding her. This was pure torment. This was no more shamming at being OK. My sister was angry and messed-up and probably going to kill us both unless she *slowed the hell down.*

'Shut up,' Jacinta hissed, cranking up the volume of the music she'd just put on. 'They're listening.'

Oh God.

'Jacinta,' I said quietly, watching the warning light on the speedometer flash – '*you are driving at an inappropriate speed for the road, please slow down* – snap out of it.'

'Shut up.'

'If you want to kill your bloody self,' I said — the speed was still climbing; I hadn't even realized the car was capable of going this fast — 'then whatever, don't bring me down with you.'

'We're going to the beach.'

'If you drive off a cliff—'

'Shut up!' Jacinta half yelled, turning round to glare at me. 'Stop always getting at me, Corin. Just *stop it.*' Jacinta's foot hit the brake, she swerved left and suddenly we'd stopped. And we were at the car park just above the beach. This was where I used to drive and sit, where I made Tom take me, where I'd been with Colton on the anniversary of our father's death. Where Jacinta had visited on the anniversary of Dad's death too.

The speed at which we'd driven here wasn't *safe.* My heart was thudding crazily. I felt like I'd just been running and running: breathless and a little dizzy.

'Get out the car,' Jacinta said, her expression hard.

I wasn't about to argue with her when she was like this.

Jacinta was making for the steps down to the beach. It was much more pleasant than the last time I'd been here. Spring was finally beginning to warm up, dry up. I followed her, my jaw slammed shut with shock and fear — I felt oddly like I was walking to my execution, like she might pull out one of those archaic guns and shoot me through the head on the sand.

'You don't understand anything,' Jacinta said, facing the sea with her arms crossed over her chest. 'You're such a kid,

Corin. You're a child. Flirting with the idea of being cynical without knowing the *consequences*.'

When she turned back towards me I realized that her eyes were slightly wet. I hadn't seen my sister cry for years. I didn't want to now. I wanted her to switch off into herself and stop talking.

'Look,' I said, 'I've had quite a bad day. Can we leave your psychotic breakdown till tomorrow?'

'Listen to me,' Jacinta said, all acute angles and rage. I didn't know whether to reach out and touch her or run the hell away. Certainly the second she let me I was going to call the hospital.

'I'm listening,' I said, swallowing back my fear.

'You are not blaming this on me,' Jacinta said. 'Our whole lives you have blamed *everything* on me and *not this time, Corin*, because this is *not my fault*. This is all yours. This. You did this.'

'It wasn't me who—'

'Shut. Up,' Jacinta said, turning round and glaring at me. She was shaking. I thought I might be too, but it was difficult to tell because my brain was numb. 'Brett *was* my carpinomen,' she said, arms still folded at right angles. 'We were soul mates. So stop pretending like you understand me, Corin. You're the stupid, silly girl who dated someone she wasn't bonded with, not me. I'm the *clever one*. I couldn't be as stupid as you if I *tried*.'

'What are you talking about?'

'Brett . . .' Jacinta's voice stopped short, and she looked back out towards the sea then took another step forward. 'He hit me.' Her face relaxed slightly, as though she'd been holding something in for *years* and *years* and finally felt able to speak.

'No.'

'Yes,' Jacinta said emphatically. 'He hit me and he manipulated me and he made me . . . he . . .'

My brain seemed to have come unstuck and was suddenly racing through a hundred things at once.

Me, pushing open the doorway and seeing those bruises from fingers pressed into her arms, believing her story about fighting with Davina at school; Jacinta pushing away her friends to be alone, wrapping her whole life around Brett as though without him she couldn't breathe. Jacinta, that helpless lacklustre expression on her face as she looked at me – as though she wanted to beg me to help her but couldn't get her voice box to cooperate. Brett, laughing and joking with me, a possessive hand curled around Jacinta's wrist.

No.

Jacinta was still talking and I didn't want to hear it.

'. . . and every time you get at me, you just—'

'Then why didn't you tell me?' I demanded. 'Why did you let me . . . ?'

Crap, I was crying. Genuine emotion choking up my throat, and Jacinta was just standing there with dried tears clotting up her eyelashes and her stony, serious expression. She hated me. Surely she must hate me. I'd hate me. I'd detest me with my whole soul, if I could; in fact, I very much thought that I *might do.*

'You were so wrapped up in your cynicism,' Jacinta said,

'you wanted to think badly of me. You *wanted* it to be my fault. You could never think of me as a victim.'

'You just let me believe . . .' I muttered, feeling all kinds of anger and regret and self-hatred bubbling up in my stomach. 'All this time and you just—'

'I couldn't take it, Corin.'

'Why didn't you just leave?' I was sobbing now, great racking tears that should have belonged to my sister but which I was borrowing; and they were shaking my shoulders and: *How long had it been since I'd cried?* Years.

'He was my soul mate,' Jacinta spat out, 'and even my *soul mate* couldn't love me. My friends just let me disappear, you hated me, Mum was distracted, Dad was dead and *even my soul mate hated me.*'

'Jacinta—'

'No, Corin. Shut up.' Jacinta was pacing across the sand now; her eyes seemed darker than normal and I wanted to reach out and collapse in her arms, but that was *her* right. 'I told you that I was going to . . . I was going to crash the car. *But I couldn't* because there was *something* that made me think that maybe I was worth a little *more* than that. So I hit the brakes. But I had to get his name off my wrist. He had to go. Every time I . . . his name *printed on my skin* when he was the one who . . . And then I did it. And they took me to hospital. And then they gave me a choice.'

I closed my hand around my own wrist guard protectively. Jacinta knew, and she was angry and she hated me and she had every right to. My sister, my poor lovely sister, who'd been trapped inside her own head for years because of some stupid *lie*.

I felt sick. I'd spent hours with the pair of them *playing* happiness, and I'd tried to flirt with him, and he'd indulged me, and the way he'd look at her and *I'd thought that was love and* . . . And the way Jacinta just *receded* into herself. She just died on cue, switching herself off so no one could hurt her.

He'd hurt her.

Oh God, that bastard had hurt my sister.

'They told me that it wasn't real,' she said, pausing as her eyes fixed on me. 'They told me that it was just a government initiative. And then they gave me a choice. Told me that there was a nice boy called Cuthbert whose Jacinta had just died in a tragic accident. They said I could become his instead, if I wanted to.'

Jacinta stepped forward and her hand closed around my arm. I tightened my grip around my wrist guard.

'What happened to Brett?'

'Incarcerated,' Jacinta said emotionlessly. 'Enough bruises to serve as evidence. Said he'd be out in forty years.'

'I'm . . . I'm sorry.'

'I went to visit him on the anniversary of Dad's death,' Jacinta said, 'after that boy grabbed me. Brett apologized.'

'Jacinta—' I managed, but then the tears cut me off. I had no right to cry. I didn't want to, either, because I didn't deserve the release of it. Still, they burned the back of my throat and bubbled up over my eyelids. My view of Jacinta distorted momentarily before a tear spilled out of my eye and down my face.

'And you,' Jacinta said, turning to stare at me, 'judging me when all the time *you've* been dating people without thinking of the consequences and treating me like I'm *stupid*. How dare you, Corin? How *dare* you? With your little cynicism clubs and your sarcasm *and you never think of the long term*.'

My sister could not have known the same thing I'd suspected for years. The idea of her, my sister, in the hospital with her wrist still in bandages as a man in a suit told her that her life was a lie. Brett was not a piece of her soul or proof that she was unlovable; just another government screw-up.

How had I let this happen?

'Then why did you turn me in?' I asked, switching over to anger in order to avoid the knifelike pain at the back of my throat and the punch of guilt to the gut. This hurt more than the knowledge that I'd had my carpinomen printed on. How had I been able to see through the intricate lies that the government had told me and not seen the fact that my sister had been hurting? Because she was right. I was honestly that willing to blame her for everything. I hadn't even *thought* of another explanation . . . I'd never even *asked* her. I just . . .

'I didn't,' Jacinta said, wrong-footed for a split second. 'What?'

'Someone handed me in,' I said. 'Don't . . . I saw you on my tabloid—'

'I heard Mum on her TTC,' Jacinta said. 'I didn't . . . I just wanted to check . . . I didn't hand you in, Corin.'

'Yes you did.'

'They offered you a choice,' Jacinta said, her voice low. 'Why the *hell* would I trust you with making that choice,

Corin? I have been breaking my *back* trying to keep you in the dark because *you* are not capable of making your own decisions.'

'That's not your decision to make,' I said, still crying. 'I never . . . *Jacinta*, I didn't want—'

'Mum turned you in,' Jacinta said, turning away from me and closing herself off. 'They got to her. I don't know how but . . . it wasn't me.'

My head was spinning.

Out of all the things I'd learned in the past twenty-four hours, this felt the most like a betrayal. I had so little faith in society at large, and in particular the government, that it barely surprised me that I'd been living in an authoritarian state (if anything, having the reasoning behind it dragged out into clarity had confused me more than the confirmation that the government stamped a name on my wrist, assigned me a career and expected me to still feel free). I could hate myself for not noticing the truth about Jacinta (which I was sure I would, probably for the rest of my life), but there was no feasible way that I could pin responsibility on her. Colton . . . that was a horrible, heavy misunderstanding that made me want to *scream* and shout, but it wasn't his fault.

But my mother . . . my mother couldn't have betrayed me to the government. My mother could not possibly have been responsible . . . she couldn't.

'Corin,' Jacinta said, her face hardening as she stared back at me. My sister was strong. I'd never realized that before . . . but she'd dealt with her own mental breakdown and Dad's death and Brett . . . how he'd hurt her . . . and she still managed to put on a brave face every single damn day. Maybe she ended up in the psych ward sometimes, buzzed up on some chemical or other, but it seemed like I didn't have a *right* to blame her for it.

I'd been wrong. I'd been so wrong I wanted to tear my own hair out. The self-hatred was beginning to really take hold now, and every single *stupid* thing I'd ever said was ringing in my ears. I'd *teased* her about Brett. I'd *provoked* her.

'Did he . . .?' I asked, blinking. 'Jacinta, when you say he hurt you, did Brett . . .?'

She ignored this. 'You found out. Mum turned you in. They took you. What did you choose?' she demanded, instead.

'Jacinta,' I said, backing away from her again, 'what did Brett do to you?'

'What did *you* do?' Jacinta asked, then her fast, clever fingers had undone the complicated catch on my wrist guard. It seemed to happen almost in slow motion, with both of us staring at my wrist as the guard fell away.

I'd seen my wrist too many damn times this past day.

Bare, exposed to the sun, and the word written there.

Colton.

I blinked.

'You cow,' hissed Jacinta.

My wrist guard fell. I dropped to the ground, scrambling to retrieve it and shake off the sand. I closed it back around my wrist and found that I was crying again.

'How could you?' Jacinta asked, wringing her hands as she returned to pacing tight circles in the sand. Her footprints overlapped and overlapped again, scattering her previous steps with each new circle of distress. 'You don't even understand what this means, Corin. They'll never leave you alone. They can ask anything and you . . . you'll just have to do it. They'll blackmail you and hurt you and—'

'What did you expect me to do?' I demanded.

'Something *sensible*, for once in your life!' Jacinta said, her eyes flashing. 'For God's sake! What, you *love* him? You're nineteen! You can't *make* that decision. What about the other Corin who's going to be alone for ever? Does that not *matter* to you? It's a test, Corin. It's just some *stupid* test to see what sort of person you are and you *failed*.'

'I don't love him.'

'Even better,' Jacinta said. 'Wonderful. What the *hell*?'

I was still crying. I hadn't even *realized* that.

'I don't,' I said, holding onto my wrist guard. 'I don't. I just . . . I wanted a choice. At least I *knew* what I was getting into. I . . . I thought it was better.'

In the heat of the moment, with Colton's expression still fresh in my brain, the whole concept of being so fully rejected by the single person I'd called a friend in years had pushed me towards the third option.

Henrik had recommended the second, which had been enough to make me want to cringe away from it . . . and that was less of a choice. That was just sitting back and letting something happen.

I'd wanted to take action. I'd wanted to show that I wasn't about to sit on this information any longer. I'd wanted him to take me *seriously* and for him to know that

I'd happily embrace my sense of choice till the end of time.

I didn't want Colton to hate me. I didn't want anything to do with some nameless, faceless Zaiden. At least Colton was a known evil. I couldn't confess to *love him* but I could say that I liked him, and that was a damn improvement on knowing nothing.

I didn't regret it. I wouldn't. No matter what Jacinta said, I wasn't going to regret the first real decision I'd ever been given.

'I thought it was better . . .' I repeated, sadly this time.

'It's not,' Jacinta spat, throwing her arms up in the air wildly. 'It's not. Congratulations, Corin, you're now a government puppet. You think they're going to let this lie? You think you're safe? Why do you think Mum handed you in? He sold you the opportunity of a choice and, as normal, you can't wait to stick a finger up at an authority figure. *You just can't help yourself.* He played you, Corin. He played you.'

'Sorry,' I said, holding my wrist guard protectively. 'What did you want me to do?'

'Not *this*,' my sister said, gesturing wildly towards my wrist. 'I didn't want you to *ruin your life.*'

'It's no more ruined than it was before.'

'Yeah?' Jacinta asked. 'You don't think the next time they want something from you they're not going to tell Colton? You think he's going to be *pleased* that you damned some poor girl to an eternal search because you *wanted a choice*?'

'Stop it.'

'No,' Jacinta said. 'You *will* face up to what you've done, Corin.'

'Well, what the hell did you want me to do?' I asked, another tear rolling down my face. The wind hit my skin, pulling it away from me. I hated crying. I hated the way it made your eyes feel *physically* vulnerable. I hated the way it clogged up in your nose and your throat and you couldn't *breathe*. I hated the way everyone could see how you felt. 'What did *you* choose?'

My sister's face contorted into a grim line. She twisted the cap on her wrist guard. She let it fall away and she pushed her wrist towards me.

And there was no name. There was nothing but the bluish hue of her veins and her pale white skin.

She had been given a choice.

And she'd been stronger than me.

Braver.

She had chosen to be alone.

For ever.

THE KISSING BOOTH – Beth Reekles

The first novel from Wattpad sensation Beth Reekles.

Meet Rochelle Evans: pretty, popular –
and never been kissed.

Meet Noah Flynn: badass, volatile – and a total player.
When Elle decides to run a kissing booth at the school's
Spring Carnival, she locks lips with Noah and her life is
turned upside down. Her head says to keep away, but her
heart wants to draw closer – this romance seems far from fairy
tale and headed for heartbreak.
But will Elle get her happily ever after?

ACID – Emma Pass

2113. In Jenna Strong's world, ACID – the most brutal,
controlling police force in history – rule supreme.
No throwaway comment or muttered dissent goes unnoticed
or unpunished. And it was ACID agents who locked Jenna
away for life, for a bloody crime she struggles to remember.

The only female inmate in a violent high-security prison,
Jenna has learned to survive by any means necessary. And
when a mysterious rebel group breaks her out, she must use
her strength, speed and skill to stay one step ahead of
ACID – and to uncover the truth about what really happened
on that dark night two years ago.

BEFORE I DIE – Jenny Downham

Everyone has to die. We all know it.

With only a few months of life left, sixteen-year-old Tessa
knows it better than most.

She's made a list though - ten things she wants to do before
she dies. Number one is sex. Starting tonight.

But getting what you want isn't easy. And getting what you
want doesn't always give you what you need. And sometimes
the most unexpected things become important.

Uplifting, life-affirming, joyous - this extraordinary novel
celebrates what it is to be alive by confronting what
it's really like to die.